Love's Fury

VIKING'S FURY BOOK 1

VIOLETTA RAND

Print Edition

Published by Dragonblade Publishing, an imprint of Kathryn Le Veque Novels, Inc

To Jeff—my love and best friend.

Our Valhalla is never far away.

And to Simon, the greatest Schnauzer and companion in the world.

TABLE OF CONTENTS

Acknowledgments

I wish to thank Kathryn Le Veque for believing in this story and me.

Star Montgomery, you are forever in my heart.

I have the greatest street team, Violetta's Valkyries. Thank you for all the love and support.

Sue-Ellen Welfonder, my fairy book godmother, hugs and kisses for all your help and encouragement.

Chapter One

Jorvik (York)
March 867 A.D.

SILVIA CLUTCHED A dozen scrolls to her chest as she raced through the scriptorium searching for somewhere to hide. She covered her mouth and coughed violently. Smoke filled every corner, diminishing the afternoon sunlight that typically filled the high-ceilinged room. Shelf after shelf of manuscripts had been obliterated by the steel axes these heathen occupiers hefted. *God's breath…* She halted. A man-beast of mythological proportions stood nearby, his attention focused on the table before him. The place where the monks passed their long days studying.

"No!" She couldn't remain silent—couldn't stop herself from screaming as he tipped the torch he held, the loose parchments providing the kindling the flames needed to spread.

She clung more desperately to her precious cargo, texts her father specifically requested she grab before he was cut down. She closed her eyes for a brief moment, stifling tears that threatened to spill, ones she'd held back so she could think clearly. But nothing helped now. How could she keep the harrowing memory of her sire's death out of her head? The answer came as goosebumps crept up her flesh like a cold wind.

She felt the weight of the intruder's stare and opened her

eyes. Had the heathen heard her yell? Or was he simply in search of something else to burn?

"Jeg er glad for å se at det er mer enn bøker i denne forlatt stedet."

His words were not lost on her. Her father had taught her enough Norse to communicate with the filthy invaders. This was no Dane, but a Norwegian. The bloody animal dared to humor himself whilst devastating her home.

"Brenn i helvete," she cursed him. *Burn in hell.*

He laughed riotously, then turned his attention back to the room.

Fool. He obviously underestimated the threat of a woman. Panic gripped her heart, but she had to remain focused. The secret tunnel running along the north wall came to mind. If she could reach it … her gaze searched for a clear route. Unfortunately, she couldn't see three feet in front of her. Nor did she know how many men were still inside. Her greatest chance of survival depended on getting out, *now.*

Silvia ran for the main entrance. She'd spent a happy childhood here—growing up exploring the buildings while her father worked. If the fire wasn't extinguished, all would be reduced to pile of smoldering rubble. A part of her soul was dying, consumed by the same flames destroying the only scriptorium in the north.

Outside, conditions weren't much better. Bodies littered the ground. Saxons—men of honor who risked their lives to reclaim their city were dead or dying. It was too late, in any case, to fight. Now mere survival would have to do. Amidst the agonizing screams and sounds of clashing metal, she hunted frantically for a place to stash the scrolls. Somewhere no one would look.

The ancient cemetery came into view. Who disturbed the dead when a city was under siege? She knew she'd done everything possible to help her father. Fulfilling his last request was all she had left to give him.

By some miracle, there was a half-dug grave nearby. It hadn't rained in days and the soil was dry. There was time to retrieve the scrolls later. She reverently laid them on the ground, unpinned her thin cloak, then knelt, wrapping the delicate papers in her mantle. Her heart pounded as she placed the bundle in the earth, then spread loose soil over it.

Satisfied they were safe, she scrambled to her feet, noting her exact location. God would lead her back here if she forgot. And if he didn't, she'd sacrifice her life trying to find it. But what now? The sanctuary appeared unharmed. *If the Vikings weren't trying to purge the northlands of holy sites, why were they targeting just the repository?* She didn't understand.

The sounds of battle grew louder...

She must find shelter. The cottage she had shared with her father was on the edge of the extensive church grounds, nearly a mile away. Vikings left nothing unsearched, no one alive—no woman untouched.

"Ikke flytt."

The deep voice cut through her like a blade and she didn't move. She should have never let her mind wander. Something sharp and hard stabbed her in the back.

"I accept your invitation."

Accept her invitation? She gasped upon remembering where she'd told him to go. *To hell.*

"Face me."

Legs as heavy as lead, she did as he demanded, dreading the moment she'd see him clearly. In the smoke filled scriptorium, he had been little more than a nightmarish shadow. But in the light, truth hit her harder than anything. Despite the soot and ash covering his face, nothing could mask his exquisite features.

Full lips—high cheek bones—a straight nose. Bronzed skin. His stark blue eyes impossible to avoid. And his hair, long and dark with coppery streaks. If she didn't stop staring, he'd misinterpret her intention, possibly rape her. Silvia tried to avert her eyes.

His axe rested against his left leg. She swallowed hard, overwhelmed by the magnitude of his presence. When he pointed across the field, toward the courtyard, she shook her head, adamantly refusing to go anywhere with him. "I'd rather die than follow you."

He growled, grabbing the top of her gown, her refusal obviously igniting his anger. The garment ripped, exposing her flesh. He gazed at her hungrily, a wicked grin splitting his face. Then his hands were on her arms, his filthy fingers digging into her skin as he shook her into submission. "Fail to obey me again and I'll strip you." He let go, shoving her backward.

She stumbled but didn't fall. If he wanted her dead, she'd be dead. If he wanted to ravish her, she would have been flailing helplessly on the ground already with her skirt hiked over her waist. Hatred flowed as freely inside her as blood. But she didn't know how to take his lack of violence.

He again pointed in the direction he wanted her to go. "Walk."

Head held high, Silvia remembered the lessons her father had painstakingly taught her over the years. Hard lessons meant for people who lived in occupied lands. Her father had said subjugation doesn't mean you must abandon pride. Christ instructed slaves to love their masters. She gritted her teeth. She'd never love a blasted Viking.

A crowd had gathered beyond the courtyard, Danes and Saxons surrounded dozens of men who were on their knees with their hands bound behind their backs. Silvia stopped short of the throng, embittered by what she knew was about to happen. Her captor gave her a little push.

"I'll tell you when to stop," he growled.

For a moment she feared she'd be forced to kneel, too. Her thoughts scattered the moment people parted and a man she well recognized, Ivarr the Boneless, son of the late king Ragnar Lothbrok, entered the circle leaning on a soldier. Battle worn and covered in dried blood, he resembled the depictions of malignant spirits in the books Silvia thumbed through in the scriptorium.

Then a sickening chant rose amongst the Vikings. *"Vi som er krigere av Odin og hans lov. Be om hjelp og har tro på ham. Med ham er vi seir."*

They dared summon Odin while standing on consecrated ground. She whispered the verse, committing it to memory so one day she could write it down. Another important skill her father had imparted—how to write in order to keep historic records. "We who are warriors of Odin and his law. Pray for help and have faith in him. With him we are victorious."

Ivarr scanned the horde, his gaze stopping on Silvia. She shifted nervously, unable to take a full breath with his eyes on her.

"Konal," the prince greeted.

Konal's fingers snaked around her elbow. He pulled her along as he stepped forward. "Everything you asked has been done, milord."

Ivarr smiled. "I never doubted you." He regarded Silvia. "Is this what you claim as your reward?"

Silvia flinched when Konal squeezed her arse. God help her, this is what she feared most. The Viking intended to make her a *thrall.* Anger pulsed through her. She'd slit her wrists first. Or disembowel him while he slept and escape. She was freeborn, the daughter of a respected scholar, not a lowborn foreigner. She pressed her lips into a tight line in an attempt to hide her emotions.

"There's enough padding to please me."

Padding? She choked back a sour laugh. There was hardly enough loose skin on her arse to pinch herself with, much less to please a bloody barbarian in bed. Oh, she knew clearly what this was all about. Growing up in a monastery offered many benefits, but it also came with a heavy price: limitless knowledge. Silvia had access to manuscripts—not all of them religious in nature. What literature the church disapproved of and confiscated often ended up in the scriptorium for monks to review. And she'd taken advantage of it, sneaking forbidden texts home where she read every word.

The prince raised his eyebrows. "Then before these witnesses," he started, "I give you … what is the *tøsen's* name?"

Konal poked her in the ribs. "Answer."

Although she'd never stood amongst so many strangers before, Silvia abandoned her civility. The Saxons kneeling at Ivarr's feet were going to be executed—they deserved to hear their kinswoman curse this murdering swine. "I pray your limbs wither, your manhood rots off, your daughters are sold into slavery, and your wife sleeps in another man's bed…"

Before Silvia closed her mouth, Konal twisted her around. His steely eyes terrified her as he squeezed her cheeks so tight she resembled a fish. Now she'd surely follow her brethren into heaven.

"This girl has cursed my manhood and honor." Ivarr broke the silence. His deep-bellied laughter inspired his men to react similarly.

She'd never meant to entertain, but to offend. To shame. The only one who appeared insulted was Konal.

"You've accepted a larger portion than you anticipated. Perhaps you want something softer to nibble on, Konal?" Ivarr's green eyes danced.

"I'll give her something to chew on," Konal shot back. "Something to..."

Ivarr raised his hand. "Be at ease brother—she's afraid. Let her stay and witness what happens to people who betray me. It will be punishment enough for her spiteful tongue."

Konal nodded, then released her on a huff. The prince's tranquil features darkened in seconds. The time for friendly banter was over and there was nothing she could do to save her kinsmen, *nothing*. The Danes were growing restless. She searched the crowd for anyone she knew. What a sad sight watching her people cower in silence. Tears stung her eyes. *God forgive her ... Lord save these innocent men.*

A loud murmur spread through the crowd as several soldiers repositioned the prisoners. The inevitable time had arrived. Silvia surged forward, hoping to reach them—to pray over them—to offer sympathy and praise for their bravery—something, anything. But Konal stopped her. His strong arm hooked her from behind, then yanked her against his inflexible body. He nuzzled her neck; his hot breath scorched her skin. She wanted to curl up and die.

"Your mind is no longer your own. You belong to me. Understand?" he hissed against her left ear. "Do not move unless I give you permission. Don't think without my approval."

More curses circulated in her stubborn mind, each filthier than the next. Words she shouldn't know; phrases unfit for the most despicable of men. Instead of speaking, she turned, then grabbed the tip of Konal's perfect nose, twisting and tugging with all her might. He let go of her. His body jerked in pain. This was the only chance she'd get.

Silvia fled.

THE LITTLE BITCH. Konal fisted his hands at his sides—laughter fueling his fury and embarrassment. Not only had she assaulted him, she'd managed to escape. He rubbed his nose as he watched her disappear around an outbuilding. Grateful Prince Ivarr hadn't witnessed any of it, Konal sucked in a breath, then strutted away from the courtyard.

He'd held his temper in check after she cursed the prince … even felt a flash of sympathy. No longer. Ivarr had a weakness for beautiful women. Not Konal—especially a Saxon witch. He'd bedded his share of dark-haired, blue-eyed beauties on both sides of the North Sea. His cock didn't do his thinking for him, only his fucking. The reason he found himself in Northumbria is because he had lost a bloody wager with his elder brother. Who could drink more mead in one night without vomiting? The punishment for his loss—serving the Danes, which did little for him. Though, he admitted, Ivarr had been a great friend and competent leader. In fairness, he'd gained lands fifty miles east of York, near the coast. And he knew exactly where he was going to take his latest acquisition.

He passed the smoldering scriptorium—laughing bitterly at the useless pursuits of monks. Then he hurried by a group of sheds and a barn. He scanned the area, no sign of her. What was her accursed name? Who was she? Why did she speak Norse and know how to curse a man so skillfully? He'd get answers and a whole lot more once he got his hands on her.

Sometime later, after kicking open door after door and searching every building he could find, Konal growled in frustration. The girl had a clear advantage. She knew where to hide. As if Odin heard his complaint, he found a monk in a garden. He wore a woolen dress, his head as smooth as a newborn's arse. As Konal approached, the man dropped his rake.

"I'll not hurt you, old man," Konal growled. "Tell me where I can find the girl who you allow in the scriptorium." As weak and incompetent as Saxons were, it surprised him that a female was permitted near the church.

The old man twisted his hands, clearly afraid.

Konal stepped closer, he expected complete cooperation. "My patience has been tested already—tell me."

"She could be anywhere."

Konal stroked his throat. At least the priest knew who he was referring to. If the holy man failed to provide the information he needed within the span of another breath, he'd split his bald head in two. "Where?" he demanded. Silence. "Answer me goddamnit, or you'll die, now."

"I'd give my life for much less," the priest challenged.

Konal lunged, seizing him by the throat, squeezing hard enough to deprive the monk of air. "At least we agree on something. Your life is worthless to me." He exerted more pressure. "Tell me."

The monk coughed uncontrollably as Konal slowly eased the pressure on his throat. "Follow the footpath west," he choked out. "Half a mile, there's a cottage surrounded by flowers and rose bushes. The girl lives there with her father. Please, don't kill her."

Konal nodded and pushed him away. "Her name?"

"Silvia."

It was not a Norse tradition to leave enemies alive. But Ivarr took pity on the residents of York so long as they submitted to his authority. Most did. And in return, the church, school, and scriptorium had been spared in the past. Northmen cared little for what gods their slaves worshipped. But not today. These ingrates had waited for the perfect moment to strike. The rebellion lead by the two deposed Northumbria kings had cost this city dearly. Hundreds had died.

The stone cottage came into view. As the priest had described, a flourishing garden ran the length of the front of the house. Konal forced his way inside, the space was dim, but he could see well enough. Two rooms downstairs, a kitchen and sitting area. The stairs probably led to a bedchamber. He climbed cautiously, listening. The door stood ajar and he entered. The small room was femininely decorated. A narrow bed with an embroidered coverlet, a table and chair, gowns laid carefully across another table. He sensed the wench's presence—the soft fragrance of flowers filled his nostrils. The same scent in her dark hair. His cock hardened instantly.

She's was here.

Perhaps hiding under the bed. He looked but found nothing. Something heavy smashed into the side of his face as he began to stand, the force of the blow enough to make his head spin. *Odin's blood.* Out of the corner of his eye, he caught a flash of movement. He spun around in time to see her retreating, but exploded sideways, snaring her ankle.

"I almost lost you," he said, still on his knees.

She kicked her hand-shackled foot, dropping the scuttle she held.

"You assaulted me with a platter?" Konal didn't know if he should laugh or beat the wench silly.

"Let me go." She kicked again, but this time, he yanked her down. He let go as she fell to the floor, the impact knocking the breath out of her.

"I suggest you get used to kneeling," Konal grabbed a fistful of her hair and dragged her toward him.

"I swear if I ever get the chance, I'll leave your lifeless form in the open so crows can feed upon your liver." Silvia thrashed like a snared rabbit.

It was a wonder that she acted so insolently. Once he regained control, he freed her hair and clamped on to her hips, flipping her over. He hovered above her face, rage and shock contorted her delicate features. Already hard with desire, her ceaseless resistance did unspeakable things to his body. But he mustn't let carnal need overshadow his duties.

She'd publicly assaulted him and cursed Prince Ivarr, a man who'd struggled in his childhood to strengthen his crippled body. A man everyone respected, for though his legs were twisted and unsightly, he could limp along. But when he sat astride a horse, he was a formidable warrior. Her words against the prince would cost any man his life. And Konal wasn't so sure she deserved to live.

Though little, she'd proven how dangerous she was if he turned his back. His duties did not include acting as a nursemaid for a bitter wench who needed a beating.

"Are you finished with your tantrum?"

In answer, she smacked his face.

All right, she thrived on violence—well so did he. Konal threw back his head and laughed. "A good thrashing makes me want you more."

"Pig!"

"And insults..." He leaned closer, harnessing her tiny wrists with one hand, then forced them over her head. "Call me whatever you wish, Silvia, I'll try to live up to each, one at a time."

She glared up at him unblinking. Her eyes were the color of the summer ocean. A mixture of sapphire and emerald, on fire with hatred. He could stare into their depths forever if he had the taste for Saxon flesh. Which he didn't. Not at the moment. But he admitted, she was no ordinary girl.

She squirmed. "Free me, *now*."

He rewarded her futile struggles with a grin. At the very least, she'd be a welcome distraction once he settled his affairs with the Danes. After a solid year of fighting, he deserved a long rest. Konal's agreement with Ivarr expired yesterday. Nothing required him to stay. Family and friends waited for him in Norway, a life he sorely missed. He weighed his options while he waited for Silvia to tire herself out. She possessed the endurance of a lad.

"Get off of me." She kneed him between the legs, grazing his *pikk*.

"Goddamnit!" He winced. The burning sensation slowly spread from his groin to his stomach. He choked down bile as he ran his fingers over her, capturing her face between his hands. With one squeeze, he could end it.

She swallowed, her eyes fixed on his lips. Although her hands were free, she didn't hit him again. "I'm going to have a taste now."

Konal lifted her and her mouth dropped open in shock, granting him access to the heat within. She tasted as sweet as the fragrance in her hair and he groaned, burning with dark lust. Did the bloody wench eat blossoms, too?

Tiny fists repeatedly connected with his chest and arms, but it didn't dissuade him. He deepened the kiss, flicking his tongue along the roof of her mouth, teasing and taunting. She went limp in his arms.

Then, as if something had changed her mind, she thrust her hands into his long hair. Konal took a chance, allowing his fingers to circle her breasts while he continued to possess her mouth. It didn't take long to find pert little nipples underneath the material of her dress. She moaned. It amused him to hear something other than a curse escape her. He cupped her breasts, which fit perfectly in his palms. Hands weary from battle, but fingers itching for pleasure. He preferred a generous bosom, the more to put in his mouth...

Whatever doubts he had before, disintegrated. He'd keep Silvia and ride her until he didn't have anything left to give. Then he'd get rid of her before he sailed home. Breaking the kiss, he rested on one elbow while running his finger lazily up the center of her body. He suspected she was covered in soft, pearly skin, honeyed to taste.

Konal suspected the sudden change in temperament was an act. No wildcat could be tamed by a kiss. His heart raced in his chest as he leaned forward and plundered her mouth again.

Chapter Two

HOLY MOTHER—SAVE ME. Fear and something else rendered her helpless when Konal kissed her. She desperately wanted to bite down on his tongue, but if she did, he'd kill her and she'd never recover the scrolls. Her only duty lie with fulfilling her oath to her father. Nothing else mattered. So she'd chosen to let the Viking do what he must.

A kiss was the last thing she'd expected, though.

After she regained her senses, she cringed. Violence hadn't stopped him. Angry words only encouraged him. She must try something else to escape his touch. "I need to relieve myself," she blurted.

Konal ceased touching her. "Aye," he said. "So must I." The desperation in his voice was unmistakable.

Did all men think this way? "I cannot provide what you need, sir."

"You are gravely mistaken, Silvia."

She rolled her eyes in annoyance. "Are you arrogant enough to think I'd willingly bed the man who axed my beloved father in the back?"

His hand fastened on her wrist angrily. "Your father?"

Now he played innocent? "You soulless bastard. I saw you in the scriptorium." Tears streamed down her cheeks.

He hauled her to her feet. His dilated pupils made his blue

eyes appear black. "Accusing me of burying my weapon in a man's back is equivalent to calling me a coward. I've never killed a man I wasn't facing. Enough bloody diversions, woman. You belong to me. And if I want you, I'll have you, willing or not."

She prayed her father had gone to Heaven, because she was sure she was headed for Hades now. "Cowards are tolerable creatures, they don't deny what they are," she said. "It's liars I hate."

He edged closer, his nose nearly brushing against her forehead. "So you've found another way to insult me?" He raised his hand midair.

Silvia squeezed her eyes shut, bracing for a blow that never came.

"Look at me, girl." He clutched her shoulders and gave her a shake.

Her eyes snapped open. "There's nothing for us to say to each other."

"Give thanks to whatever gods you pray to. If you were a man, I'd break your neck."

"While facing me or from behind?"

His explosive snarl made her legs tremble. She'd never seen an expression so menacing on a man's face before. But he wasn't a man, only a baseborn animal with enough intelligence to speak.

"You'll leave this house with me. But I give you fair warning—consider how you'll go. Upright or flung over my shoulder."

She felt stupid. Afraid. Weak. Whether he swung the weapon that killed her father or not, he was equally responsible for his death. Hatred swelled inside her. "*Dra til helvete.*"

"Accepted—only this time, you'll show me the way." In one swift move, Konal hoisted her over his shoulder.

Her screams didn't deter him as he carried her outside.

Panic set in as Silvia realized where he was taking her, back to the courtyard. She writhed, kicked, and beat her fists against his back in protest, but the lecherous whoreson only tightened his grip.

"Put me down," she demanded.

"I gave you a choice, remember?" he asked.

Her blood chilled. He possessed no feelings whatsoever. The bastard murdered her father and knew she was suffering, yet was determined to increase her pain. He would do anything to win. Do anything to prove she had no control of her own life. But she'd not give in. Not while she could still draw a breath. Silvia dug her fingernails into the soft flesh of his earlobe.

"*Drit!*" He stopped abruptly, slapping her arse so hard her teeth rattled. "The next time you assault me, I'll tie you hand and foot."

She cried out as he shrugged her off his shoulder. Once her feet hit the ground, she started to run, but he grabbed a fistful of her gown. Silvia was no match for his brute strength.

"Don't you have a drop of mercy in your soul?" she asked.

"Mercy?" His brows knit together as if he didn't know what she meant. "I'll ask the questions."

Silvia bit down on her tongue to keep herself from cursing him again. Resisting was hopeless. She glanced down at the dirt-caked toes of her shoes. "Stop dragging me, *please*."

"Stop fighting." He relinquished his hold on her dress.

She straightened her gown, frowning at the large tear near her shoulder. "Why are we going back to the church?"

Konal's mouth thinned. "To witness the executions of the men who committed treason."

Silvia gasped as terror squeezed her chest. "You'd force me to watch after all the unspeakable cruelty I've already endured?

Have you no heart? Not a shred of compassion for a woman whose father has been taken away from her?"

"Woman," he uttered, "if you knew my true nature, you'd understand how much I've held back already."

She believed him.

"I've permitted you to live this long for only one reason."

Aware of his meaning, she didn't press him any further.

"You'll walk with me to the courtyard in silence. Accept your bitter portion of responsibility for the assault your former king led against Prince Ivarr. When the executions are over, we will return to your cottage, gather your belongings, and leave. Understand?"

Inwardly, she'd never agree to anything he demanded, but she nodded.

Before they reached the courtyard, the unmistakable sound of weeping and wailing assaulted her ears. Silvia halted. Unshed tears burned her eyes. She couldn't go on, didn't want to see the bloodshed. Konal squeezed her arm and forced her to keep moving. She swallowed a scream when they approached the yard. Dozens of bodies swung from the trees.

The overwhelming stench of death nearly made her faint. Of all the unholy methods of torture and execution, she'd never conceived of so many men being killed at the same time. Her heart ached as she forced herself to look away, only to find Prince Ivarr standing in the forefront. She imagined ripping his sword from his hip and gutting him from neck to navel.

Saxon women and children were huddled together to her right—the mothers, wives, sons, and daughters of the deceased. To her left, the Danes celebrated, drinking wine, beating their swords against their shields, and praising their bloodthirsty leader. She backed away, wanting to put as much distance between her and the occupiers as she could. The safest place to wait was next to the only heathen who showed any restraint, Konal.

Surely all the rebels had been executed. Why the soldiers were still assembled she didn't know. Silvia waited for Ivarr to disperse them. Instead, he raised his hands, signaling for attention. Her unsteady gaze shot over Ivarr's shoulder. The Danes' fierce countenances were forever imprinted in her mind. Godless, lawless fiends. She'd seen death a hundred times today, yet the prince's face frightened her more. Something flickered in his eyes as he turned away.

Three soldiers, dragging a chained man in their wake, entered the square.

"Have I not been generous?" Ivarr asked. "See how my leniency has been repaid. I entrusted this city to an honorable man—a Saxon—good King Ecgberht—only to be besieged the day I return after spending a year in the field. You Saxons worship a god who proclaims peace and goodwill toward men. What goodwill have you shown me?"

Silence.

"This man," Ivarr continued, pointing at the prisoner now kneeling at his feet, "is no ambassador of peace. He's a murdering tyrant whose subjects abandoned him. In my absence, he incited a rebellion, joined forces with enemies of my late father, who he cast into a pit of snakes to die like an animal."

His accusations awakened the throng. *"Ragnar, Ragnar, Ragnar..."*

A chill spiraled down Silvia's spine. He spoke truthfully. Aelle was a despot ruler, never endorsed by the Church, and never a friend to the commoners. Until today. He'd made peace with his enemies and launched an offensive on behalf of the people—on behalf of God.

"I hear the cries of the slaughtered, thousands of souls

whose blood is on Aelle's hands, not mine. The only goodwill I'll give you this day is the end of my sword." He backhanded the former king so hard, he fell sideways. "Allfather demands justice. I demand vengeance."

Ivarr unsheathed his weapon, gripped the handle between both hands, raised his arms vertically above his head, and then drove the blade into the earth. "Place him on all fours."

"No!" Silvia shook her head in disbelief. She understood Ivarr's bloodlust. But not this way. Not blood eagle. They'd cut his ribs along the spine, breaking them so they resembled bloody wings, then extract his lungs through his back. She faced Konal. "He is your friend. Stop him." Her body trembled uncontrollably. "I beg you, milord. Do this one thing for me and I will submit to your every demand." She fell to her knees, staring up at him. "Please."

His features darkened. "I cannot interfere."

"I'm offering to serve you unquestioningly—I'll willingly become your slave."

"You assign too much value to yourself, girl."

"Do I?" She raised her chin. "Then why did you follow me?"

"I did what I had to do."

She barely had time to think about his reply before Aelle shrieked. Dreading what she'd see if she turned, Silvia stood up, still facing Konal. "I ask—" Another nightmarish howl came. "Dear God." She swung around. No words could describe the sight. None. Aelle's pain became hers—it stabbed her heart. She staggered forward a few steps. "I suspect not even your gods could favor this torment," she called over her shoulder.

Something akin to rage boiled up inside her. If she didn't have the courage to ask for mercy on behalf of a fellow Christian, no matter how despised he'd been, then what was left to live for? God judges hearts, not men.

"You'll die half the man you were born…" Ivarr promised.

She stopped several yards away, her mouth opened, then closed. She couldn't find her voice to scream, or tear her glance away from the bones protruding from Aelle's mutilated body. The world began to spin. She started to sweat profusely, then clutched at her chest as she lost her footing. "Not now…"

Everything went dark.

Chapter Three

SOMETHING DIDN'T FEEL right. Warmth and silence aren't what Silvia expected when she opened her eyes. Nor did she foresee waking up in the comfort of her room. Two candles burned low on the stand in the corner of her bedchamber. The vessel she placed fresh flowers in yesterday had been moved to the large table near her bedside along with a cup of wine and a plate of bread. Was she dreaming? Of course the pulsing pain in the back of her skull provided what proof she needed that she wasn't. She had, indeed, survived. Watched her father fall, been claimed by Konal, and witnessed the deaths of too many Saxons to count.

She groaned as she sat up and then kicked the thick fur off her body.

Someone had removed her tattered gown and replaced it with a clean chemise. Konal? The man who scarred her country with fire and war? The man who forced her to watch King Aelle die? The cold-hearted bastard who told her she could no longer think or speak without his permission? She laughed out loud. Where was he? Her father slept on a pallet in the main room belowstairs. The thought of Konal's body touching the same coverlets her father used angered her.

She slid out of bed, then cautiously crept downstairs. Konal was sprawled on a chair with his feet propped against the hearth.

She smelled stew and eyed the roaring fire. The food was likely made from the rations the priests gave her father. Payment for his invaluable services. She glared at Konal. He looked so peaceful and *vulnerable*. Even warriors required sleep. She'd fantasized about this moment, but never expected it to come so soon.

Sharp utensils were kept in a drawer in the kitchen. If she could sneak past him and get a knife—she'd slit his throat. Her need for blood surprised her. Would she belong to the devil if she killed him? It didn't matter. Hades had come to her dressed as a Viking. And she had every right to defend herself and avenge her father's death.

Once in the kitchen, she chose the knife her father had used to cut meat. She admired the sleek metal blade, planning to stick it between his ribs. But murder went against everything she'd been taught, and though her heart had been hardened against the Danes, she still wrestled with her conscience. In order to follow through, she needed to forget the benedictions the priests had taught her. Abandon Christ's message.

She approached Konal from behind. He slept so deeply, assuring his death would be swift and painless.

Edging around the chair, she held the knife flush against her thigh. She should be disgusted by him, but instead, she pitied his vile existence. Beasts stalked and killed their prey, driven by instinct. What if the Vikings were no better—didn't understand what they did was an abomination to God. Her mouth went dry. Cruelty dwelt inside him and she was sure his hands would never aid the cause of goodness and charity. There was nothing worth sparing. Nothing. She raised her hand above her head and her gaze dropped from his face to his chest. His heart—she'd stab him in the heart.

AS THE BLADE came down, Konal pried it from her hand.

"Piercing a man in his sleep is the same as stabbing him in the back." Although he'd been watching her the whole time, he wanted to see if she'd actually do it. He gritted his teeth. He'd never sleep with both eyes closed again if she were around.

"What do you know of honor?" She lunged, wrapping her tiny hands around his wrist. When he raised his arm, her feet left the ground. "Give me the knife. Let me kill you."

His jaw relaxed as he pondered her words. "Not today." He yanked his hand free and the knife clattered to the floor. Scrambling to get to it before he did, Konal tackled her, pinning her down. He wrestled her hands behind her back. "Yield."

"I ... I can't breathe with you on top of me."

He laughed bitterly. "If you can speak, you can breathe."

"Why are you here? What do you want from me?" She kicked her feet.

A question he refused to answer. Instead, he turned her over. Now their faces were inches apart. Her heart thundered against his chest and fear flashed across her face. Those eyes—Odin curse them—were too hypnotizing to look away from.

He should wield his power over her by bedding her so she'd never forget her place again. She'd assaulted him more times than he cared to remember. What punishment should he give? How could he convince her to obey without physically breaking her? Any other woman would have tasted his wrath. But there was something about this wench that intrigued him.

Someone knocked on the door, and before Konal could say anything, it opened.

"I know you haven't bedded a woman in a long while, but don't you have to take your breeches off to fuck?" a familiar voice barbed.

The insult grated his nerves, but he turned far enough to

catch a glimpse of his cousin standing in the doorway. Silvia bucked. "Enough," he commanded, glowering at her. He rolled off her, stood, then raked his fingers through his hair. She scooted away, still hunched on the ground. "Get up."

"Do you need help?" his cousin asked.

"Shut up, Hallam." The wench had embarrassed him already. He turned his attention back to her. "Do you yield?"

She stared up at him, chin raised defiantly. He'd wait one heartbeat longer for her to answer properly before he hoisted her off the floor. "My patience is waning—speak."

Hallam chuckled. "Maybe if you stop growling like a bear and give the girl a moment to collect herself…" his cousin started. "She's earned the admiration of a few Danes—nothing to be overly proud of if you ask me."

"Admiration?" Konal's lips thinned with annoyance. "For what?"

"For blaspheming the prince."

Leave it to a bloody Dane to approve of their leader being cursed. Backward thinking fools. "I wonder what he would have done if she kicked him in the bollocks," Konal shot back, remembering his own pain.

"What you were attempting, *without* braies."

Konal held back a bitter laugh. It bothered him to think the Danes admired anything he owned. He eyeballed Silvia again. Though she hadn't responded, she remained quiet on the floor. He focused on his cousin. "Why are you here?"

"Do I need a reason to visit my kinsman?"

Konal's brows shot up. "The last time you darkened my door, I lost a wager."

"I remember." Hallam shrugged nonchalantly. "All the more reason for you to celebrate." He pulled a scroll from his cloak. "Prince Ivarr sends his blessings—your discharge papers."

Freedom stared him in the face.

Konal waved his cousin inside. "There's wine and stew."

Hallam followed him to the hearth, throwing questioning looks at the girl. "Where shall I sit? The floor looks exceedingly comfortable."

Konal scoffed. "You'll sit on the chair." He pointed. "And you," he addressed Silvia. "Serve us, *now.*" When she didn't move, he dropped his hands to his sides, frustrated at her continued disobedience. She wasn't acting the way she was supposed to. "So help me," he bellowed. "If I have to move from this spot, I'll use your body in ways you never imagined possible."

Finally, she jumped up and scuttled into the kitchen.

Konal took the scroll from his cousin, broke the wax seal, and then opened it. He scanned the document, searching for the prince's signature and a legal description of the lands he'd been given. As he'd expected, 3,000 acres were his to do with as he pleased. "Thank you for this." He folded the paper in half, then placed it on the stone mantel.

"Where will you go?"

"I need to spend some time looking over my new assets," Konal started, rubbing his beard while he gazed toward the kitchen. "From what I've been told, the Saxons who manage the house are very capable and welcome the change in ownership." He sat down.

Silvia returned carrying a tray. She stopped in front of Hallam first, offering him a cup of wine. Then she addressed Konal. "Drink, milord?"

This is what he envisioned the girl doing, serving him without complaint. He nodded, accepting his measure. She set the tray on the nearby table, walked to the hearth with two bowls, and ladled stew into one. She presented his cousin with a bowl.

Hallam smiled, then tasted the food.

"Venison," he commented, licking his lips.

"Seasoned with my father's wine," Silvia added, returning with Konal's portion.

Konal held out his hand. "Good girl."

She stared down at him, her hands trembling.

"You've nothing to fear," Konal said sincerely.

Her eyes flared, then she dumped the hot food on his lap. "It's not fear, milord."

Konal howled in pain, shooting up from his chair. Burned. *Goddamn it.* The creature was determined to maim his manhood. "You'll pay..." He shook his fist at her as she ran abovestairs. Her bedchamber door slammed shut. "Wretched bitch."

Hallam's laughter didn't help.

Konal looked down. His blasted braies were covered in dark broth, chunks of meat, and vegetables. He brushed himself off. "There's less frost between Bestia's legs than hers."

"And I thought the war was over..." Hallam said.

Konal lowered his chin. "She's a madwoman. Raised with wolves. Possessed by spirits." The shock hadn't abated yet.

"If she's unbendable—sell her."

Konal knew *who* was prepared to pay and gritted his teeth. Hallam couldn't keep his eyes off her. The girl's features weren't exactly Saxon. She favored the Norse in some ways. Dark-haired with eyes that penetrated his soul. No wonder the Danes prized her. She was a walking, breathing Valkyrie who made him feel like an animal. A rabid one.

Chapter Four

PUNISHMENT, SEVERE—SWIFT—PAINFUL—UNFORGETTABLE. THAT'S what the wench deserved and that's what she'd get for her latest act of violence and disobedience. Konal paced in front of the fire, collecting his thoughts. Cursed Saxon.

"The longer you delay the sale and tolerate her continued defiance, the more likely she is to make an utter fool out of you."

"You, too, need to be reminded of your place, cousin," he growled. "Forget anything you've dreamt of doing with her. The only man she'll have any dealings with is me."

Hallam stood, placed his empty bowl on the table, then walked over to his cousin. "You think I'm acting selfishly? Devised a plan to relieve you of your captive for my own pleasure?"

"I don't think," Konal emphasized. "I know. History speaks for itself." A skilled scavenger, Hallam spent his youth traipsing after Konal, drinking and fighting at his side—benefitting from his leftovers. "You can assure the Danes I've completed my service and am thoroughly pleased with my reward. Leave me. Now."

Hallam gave him an appraising look. "I thought you were in a rush to return home."

Konal shrugged. "Today, tomorrow, a few weeks hence, it

matters not. I'll leave when I'm ready. After I've fucked some sense into that witch upstairs."

His cousin smiled unconvincingly. "If it's female companionship you require," he said. "There is a house full of more willing partners..."

"I'll warn you once, Hallam. Continue to harass me and you'll pay the price." He balled his fists at his sides, his nails digging into his palms. "Go. I'll send for you before I leave for the coast."

"You're very charming when you're angry." Hallam headed for the door. "I respect your wishes. But, promise me one thing."

One thing usually meant two or three. "What?"

"If you ever grow tired of her, I'm the only man you'll consider selling her to."

Konal squared his shoulders. Hallam knew how to get under his skin. How to enrage him enough to beat him to death. Seven years ago, it nearly happened, that's when everything changed between them. The only reason he'd escaped Konal's wrath ... Hallam's father intervened. It earned him the title—Konal the Red. "Get out."

His kinsman bowed with mock respect, then disappeared outside.

Konal turned his attention to the narrow stairs. Blood pounded between his ears. He massaged his temples and took several deep breaths. *Odin's blood.* The list of grievances he had against the girl outnumbered all enemies he'd killed. She'd tweaked his nose, cursed the prince, kicked him in the bollocks, tried to stab him, and now burned him with hot stew. All in front of his kinsmen. He climbed the first step slowly, then found himself taking two at a time. When he reached the landing, he kicked the door open.

Silvia didn't move from her spot on the bed.

Much to his surprise, she appeared completely unaffected by his sudden intrusion. "Woman," he hissed. "I've come to impart a valuable lesson."

"You've nothing to teach me, barbarian," she retorted. "Except how to hate."

"Hate?" he repeated as he neared her bedside. "I've shown you everything *but* hatred. Do you agree?"

She averted her eyes.

"Haven't I?" he asked more heatedly, curling his fingers under her chin and forcing her to look up at him.

She jerked away. "Don't touch me unless you plan on killing me."

No fear. No sense. "You'll pay for your disrespect."

"If it is coin you want, I have silver." She slid off the bed, walked to a cabinet, and took out a leather pouch. She whirled around. "Here is my life savings. It should be enough to buy my freedom." She flung the bag at him.

It hit him in the chest, then fell to the floor. Yet another assault. Perhaps the girl was deranged. That would explain her careless resistance. Konal had never met a woman with so little regard for her own life. It baffled him. What could he do to a woman who'd lost her mind? Imprison her, starve her to death? Fit her with an iron collar and chain? Sell her to an expectant fool like Hallam? *No...*

The thought of another man touching her nearly drove him mad. He swept her into his arms and dropped her like a sack of grain on the bed. The wood frame creaked and then collapsed. She squealed, rolling into the middle of the now sagging mattress. She thrashed her arms and legs in a pitiful attempt to get up. He bellowed with laughter at how helpless she looked, then leaned over and grabbed two fistfuls of the front of her dress. He'd made up his mind.

"It's time," he said without remorse, before lifting her.

She attempted a wild punch, but missed his face. "Let me go!"

Never. His rage turned to intrigue. Taming wild creatures had always been a favorite pastime growing up—breaking horses—domesticating boars he trapped in the woods. Why should he see her any differently? She behaved savagely—he'd treat her thusly. Still holding on to her dress with both hands, he dragged her kicking and screaming to the nearest chair and then sat down. He pulled her onto his lap, flipping her onto her stomach.

With one arm hooked around her neck, he hiked her skirt above her waist.

"No! Dear God, no!" She reached behind her back, clawing his arm.

"Well time somebody taught you to respect your master." Konal eyed her round, little arse appreciatively. Pearly white cheeks begged for his attention. Crack. His hand came down hard. She screamed. Crack. She flailed.

"Stop, *please*," she cried.

Thwack.

"No..." She kicked her feet.

He landed a series of stinging blows. A few making him wince. Finally, her quiet sobs stopped him. He eyed her backside, satisfyingly red. "Have I made my point clearly?"

"Godless bastard," she said.

Smack. "Had enough?"

"I hate you."

Crack. "Will you obey me?"

Silence.

He nodded then and, thinking she finally understood, he let

go. "Get up."

Silvia rolled off, dropping onto the floor.

"After everything you've done, a simple thrashing has silenced you like a child. Collect yourself woman, I'm still hungry."

That made her move. She hoisted herself up and rearranged her skirt. Her beautiful face was tear-stained, her eyes swollen and red. "Then feed yourself."

Should he get a horsewhip? "Get me a bowl of stew and some wine, *now*." Blowing out a gusty breath, Konal swore the gods were testing him, perhaps even enjoying his suffering.

"I refuse to serve you. I won't be forced to spend another bloody moment in your presence."

"Do you truly have a death wish?"

"If it reunites me with my beloved father," she said, "I freely offer you my throat."

Stunned, he stared at her. Her impudence seemed endless. Konal moved his hand to his weapon belt where he kept a blade for moments like this. Slitting the throat of an enemy had always been a quick, clean way to dispose of someone. Should he fulfill her wish? Send her to whatever underworld she believed in? Reunite her with her sire? In his lifetime, he'd only been forced to kill one woman. The old bitch threatened to poison his sister. Although he'd been justified, he felt so guilty afterward that he paid a generous *wergild* to the woman's family.

"Please," she pleaded. "Spare me the wait."

He started to unsheathe the blade, but something stopped him. A memory from his childhood. A terrifying feeling that grew inside him. The thought of her dying—the idea that he'd ever hurt her intentionally—nearly dropped him on his knees. Beads of sweat formed on his forehead. What would keep him from carrying out her wish? Saxons were as numerous as cattle but worth much less.

"I'll not kill you today. Or any other bloody day you choose." He'd hear no more of it.

Her features twisted into the blackest look he'd ever seen on a woman's face. "First you whip me into submission and now you refuse to kill me?" She shook her head. "I don't understand. A Norseman with a conscience? Can it be true?" Bitterness dripped from her sweet lips.

He'd had enough. Konal grabbed her around the waist and tugged her to his chest. This is what she did to him; the reason he refused to maim or kill her. Instead of hurting Silvia, he'd dominate her. Break her. Have her if it was the last thing he ever did. He ignored her protests and captured her angry mouth with his. One taste. He thrust his tongue between her lips, taking what he'd wanted all along.

She melted in his arms.

Then he broke away and chuckled—not wanting her to see how much she affected him. Her eyes grew wide with confusion, but he didn't care. He'd found her weakness. "Before you join me in the morning, I suggest you find a way to control your temper. If you don't, I'll be forced to flog you in front of every Dane I can find."

He left her standing in the middle of her bedchamber.

ASHAMED OF HERSELF, Silvia dipped a cloth in the pitcher of water by her bed and wiped her traitorous lips clean. She enjoyed the kiss this time, and however brief the pleasure didn't matter. It infuriated her. She scanned the room. Everything was out of place. Her bed appeared unfixable. The contents on top of the table near her bed were on the floor. And her silver… By God, the fiend refused to take her money. Why? She walked across the room and picked up the leather bag. She squeezed it so hard it hurt.

If only it were his thick neck between her hands. She'd choke the life out of him. The man she suspected killed her father. The animal who dared to assault her under her own roof. She rubbed her arse. It stung. How much torture could she withstand? She gazed down at her dress. Ruined. Her whole world was breaking apart and tears filled her eyes. She'd warred with herself long enough. Since she survived the fire in the scriptorium, the public executions, every attack she'd made against Konal, and because he refused to kill her, she'd have to take matters into her own hands. In the morning, after she broke bread, she'd sneak into the kitchen, take a knife, slip back upstairs, say her prayers, and slit her own throat.

Hope for a dignified death disappeared the moment her father died. Once he shut his eyes and breathed his last, her soul went with him. Life withered in that moment. All that remained was a shell of the woman she had been. She'd brave an eternity in fire to escape the living, breathing devil downstairs.

The bastard was eating her father's food and sleeping on his chair. Silvia couldn't banish the appalling image from her mind. Norsemen were soulless creatures. More frigid than the regions they sailed from. And once she was gone, he'd steal everything. The legacy of her family wiped from the minds and hearts of her kinsmen forever.

She flung herself on the floor and wept bitterly. For her father, the mother she never knew, and now God. Whatever sins she'd committed to deserve this level of suffering she didn't know. But she'd end it soon enough.

Chapter Five

BRIGHT SUNLIGHT FILTERED through the small windows in the main room of the cottage. Konal groaned; he wasn't ready to get up. Surprisingly, the wench stayed abovestairs for the remainder of the night. And once he felt comfortable, he allowed himself to fall asleep on the floor in front of the hearth. However, before he laid down, he surrounded himself with all the furniture he could find. If she attempted another attack, she'd have to break through his defenses first.

He staggered to his feet, rubbing his eyes. His stomach rumbled. He could have eaten last night, but decided to wait for Silvia to serve him this morning. She'd proven a worthy opponent, but her iron will was no match for his strength. He grabbed a pitcher of water from the table and walked to the kitchen. Linens were folded neatly on a shelf. He wet a cloth and then cleansed his face and neck. It felt good to wipe the dirt and grit away. He'd gone too long without a bath, and once he returned to Norway, he'd spend a month in the bath house.

Throwing the linen down, he peered around the cramped space. A counter ran the length of the opposite wall where he spotted two loaves of bread. Baskets of oats and barley were nearby, alongside a trencher containing dry fish. Then he found a large bowl of beans and a bowl of dates. Plenty of food to last several days, enough for the girl to cook with.

"Milord..."

He turned at the sound of her voice. At first he felt contempt, but he couldn't stay angry for long. Not with the way she looked—her long hair combed to a lustrous shine and a blue gown on with a fitted bodice that more than accentuated her generous breasts. She'd taken the time to make herself presentable, which suggested a change of heart. Perhaps she finally accepted her new life. "Did you sleep?"

"Enough to realize how foolish I've been."

He shouldn't allow himself to soften with pity, but he knew the lingering pain of losing someone he loved or admired. War and plague had darkened his life many times. If the girl cooperated, he'd treat her decently. And once he was ready to sail home, he'd give her to a man he trusted. She couldn't expect a better situation.

She slipped past him, grabbing the basket of barley. "Shall I make something to eat?"

"Aye," he answered, watching her closely. He'd been taught at an early age to question everything, especially if it seemed too good to be true. A sound whipping provided discipline, but with a temperament like hers, he found her transformation hard to accept. "Tell me why the priests permit a woman to live here."

"Is my life truly of interest to you?" She wet her lips with her irresistibly pink tongue.

"I expect an answer."

"Before the king confiscated my family's lands, my father served as a tutor for the sons of the northern lords. The priests took pity and offered him a position as a scribe. This is the only home I've ever known."

She moved away, taking ingredients from a shelf and a pot from a cabinet. "If you thought to find anything worth stealing, milord, I assure you, there's nothing of great value in this cottage. My father's wealth disappeared with his estate. We rely on whatever the bishop gives us for food. And my father's salary hardly covers our expenses."

He believed her. "Your mother?"

She stopped working, staring at him through narrowed eyes. "Dead."

"When?"

"The day I came into the world."

He nodded with understanding. She'd not come to terms with the death of her mother yet. "We've something in common then. My mother perished three days after giving birth to my only sister, her fifth babe." Konal stepped forward hoping to provide some comfort, but she avoided his arms. "I will not hurt you."

Her protective stance conveyed her mistrust. "You demanded *certain* things last night. I'll cook and clean, but I'll be damned before I let you paw me like a common whore."

He glared at her. She'd do whatever he wanted. And if it included providing the physical relief he needed, he'd strip her naked. "Do you really think anything you say or do will keep you from my bed if that's where I wish you to be?"

Laughter followed his question. "I've never bedded a man," she informed him bitterly. "My body is sacred."

Sacred? Konal chuckled. "See what comes from living in the shadow of a monastery? Bloody Saxon priests fill women's heads with lies." Only the nobility could afford such luxuries. Virtue had no place in her world if her body could provide the means for her support and protection. "I suggest you forget whatever dreams you grew up with. Your new life is staring you in the face, girl. I'll decide what's best for you. And remaining a virgin isn't part of it."

Silvia stiffened. "You've already stolen my dignity." She

thrust a hand on her hip. "Now you threaten my chastity."

"There's no shame in sharing my bed," he said. "I'm a celebrated warrior—most women would be honored..." She let her gaze stray to his chest, then below his waist. "See," he said. "Your curiosity betrays you."

She immediately snapped her head up. "You misinterpret my actions, milord."

At the very least, Konal appreciated her wit. "Do I now?"

She retreated a step. "My wandering eyes don't signify admiration."

"What then?" He'd play her game for the moment.

"I don't understand why women find you so irresistible," she said smugly. "You're not fit for a Saxon barn."

He growled, then scuffed forward, snaring her delicate wrist. "Let me show you what kind of a beast I truly am." His bollocks ached more than he cared to admit. Weeks without female companionship had left him desperate. And every time Silvia was within sight, his cock stood at attention. Her inescapable sensuality attracted him. "Your resistance increases my desire tenfold."

Her unblinking eyes challenged him. "Your unnatural desires don't frighten me. I care nothing for your murdering, heartless soul. You'll die a violent death and rot in hell like all your kind. Your disdain for everything honorable and pure cannot deprive me of my faith."

Konal held her gaze.

"Even watching my former king die like a pig at slaughter cannot silence me. Only one thing devastates me more than my father's death."

Her conviction was admirable, but it wouldn't change her fate. "Tell me."

"Your cowardice."

The words struck as deadly as a dagger. Konal let go of her arm. *Coward?* Anger ripped through him. "You can't possibly know what you're saying. Recant."

She shook her head. "Truth can never be retracted."

SHE'D BAITED HIM on purpose, attacked his sense of honor and courage in hopes of making him hate her. If she died a maiden, perhaps God would forgive her for taking her own life. As impenetrable as Konal acted, his ego appeared as soft as a woman's body. Something she'd learned the hard way after years of subjugation to the Danes. Saying the wrong thing had cost many Saxons their lives. This one refused to kill her—but if she openly questioned his honor and bravery—he'd prove himself.

"Truth is subjective," he muttered. "Your insult is undeserved."

"Is it?" she asked incredulously. "You murdered my father. A peaceful, defenseless man. In my country this suggests cowardice."

"Don't say it again." He slowly backed her up to the wall. "I *should* kill you." He loomed threateningly, all heat and rage. "I didn't slay your sire, Silvia."

His intense blue gaze nearly shattered her resolve. A strange feeling stirred deep inside her belly. Something told her to stop pushing him, to believe him. But she deafened herself to whatever inner voice was trying to change her mind. "Prove yourself to me."

He slammed his fists against the wall on either side of her face. It frightened her, so she closed her eyes, willing him away. When she opened them again, he was still staring at her.

"I'm a fool for ever thinking you'd be obedient." He shook

his head. "Where I found you should have served as a warning. Women don't belong in the places where men seek knowledge." He retreated then and started to pace in front of her.

She wisely kept her place, giving him time to clear his mind.

"How many languages do you speak?" he asked.

"Five."

"How many manuscripts have you read?"

"Too many to count."

"Do you write?"

"Yes."

He raked his fingers through his hair, his expression menacing. She'd pushed him too far. "I've heard that in your country a woman has the right to ask a man to prove himself before he wins her hand. Have you no respect for your own customs?" She did her best to mask the tremor in her voice.

"You're a prize won in battle. Not a woman whose heart I wish to conquer. Yet you ask me to prove myself worthy. And if I refuse?" He pounded his fist against his chest.

She raised her chin. "Then shame will follow you wherever you go—even to the ends of the earth."

"It seems we cannot agree," he said, frustrated. "I have every right to bed you, but will not have my honor questioned."

Praise God. Silvia sighed with relief. She hated having this beast in her house. The tactic she'd utilized had the same effect on him as castration. There'd be no lovemaking before or after breakfast. "Shall I finish making our pottage?"

"I've half the appetite," he said severely. On a huff, he left the kitchen without telling her what to do.

She continued to prepare the morning meal, using crushed almonds to thicken the mixture. Next, she cut several slices of bread and placed them on a tray. She'd get through one meal and then carry out her plan.

While the porridge bubbled in the pot, she listened carefully for Konal. She'd never felt so ragged and frightened in her life. But after Konal whipped her yesterday and she'd shed every last tear, something changed inside her. The only way she could describe it, her fear retreated—enabling her to think more clearly.

The scrolls… She wiped the sweat from her forehead with the back of her hand. What about the precious manuscripts her father had entrusted her with? His last words weren't a confession or filled with love as another man's would have been. That's what set him apart from others. God's work took precedence. And she'd be damned before she failed to get those parchments safely into the right hands.

"Woman!"

Silvia spooned a large portion of cereal into his vessel, then spit in it. Placing two bowls onto the same tray with the bread, she then walked into the main room determined to get the scrolls before the day ended.

Chapter Six

KONAL WATCHED SILVIA slowly eat the miniscule amount of pottage in her bowl. She looked nervous hunched in the chair at the far end of the table. He supposed it would have been impossible to convince her to sit near him. "Are you all right? Eat a slice of bread."

She sighed. "Short of ramming it down my throat, milord, I'll risk your displeasure by refusing."

He leaned his head on his hand and stared at her. In Norway, every living thing was eager to please him out of respect. In Northumbria, he couldn't get a woman to comply with his simplest wish. The gods had sent him good fortune up until this point. "I am needed in the village today," he said. "If I let you stay here, I expect you to pack your belongings in preparation for our departure tomorrow."

She gazed at him. "Where are we going?"

"East. To my lands." He pushed his chair back and then stood. "If you try to escape again, I'll fit you with a slave collar and chain. Trust me when I say it won't be a pleasant experience to be paraded around the public square like a dog on a leash."

She nodded silently, perhaps thinking what she would look like.

"And when nighttime comes," he added, "you'll be stripped naked and bound to my bed."

She cleared her throat. "That's how you've gained favor with women, forcing yourself upon them." She clicked her tongue reprovingly.

He felt his patience slipping. "You'll change your mind after you've slept with me."

"If you're in such an all-fire hurry to have me, why not clear the bloody table and take me now?"

He eyed the tabletop, then swallowed as his throat and braies tightened at the same time. Frustration settled over him. There was definite danger in her strategy. She knew he couldn't have her until he proved himself. Before she'd spoken her latest challenge, he'd accepted the fact that he'd have to wait to bed her. No longer, she'd get her wish. He'd complete her blasted task and have her before dawn. "Name your price."

"My price?" Her eyes narrowed to blue slits. "I'm not for sale."

His palms burned. Another spanking would help her immensely. "Speak your challenge, woman."

"Bring me the head of the man who murdered my father."

She'd answered so quickly. No doubt she had this planned from the moment he claimed her. *"Månen og stjernene ville være lettere å oppnå."*

"You speak English well enough, milord."

"The moon and stars would be easier to achieve," he growled in her native tongue. She had nothing to lose at this point by demanding something so outrageous. "You are not worth the life of one of Prince Ivarr's men."

She had the eyes of an angry child. "Then I believe *you* guilty of the crime."

He didn't answer.

"I welcome your resistance, milord." She started to gather the dirty dishes. "The longer you delay, the longer I'm safe from your carnal desires." Without looking back, she disappeared into the kitchen.

Konal didn't give her the pleasure of a response. He opened the door and stepped outside. Wretched little creature. Structure and discipline defined his life. He took meals and went to sleep at the same time every day unless he was in the field. The girl disrupted his schedule—shamed him in ways no man would be permitted to do.

As he walked, it started to rain. He welcomed it and hoped his new lands were fertile. Before he returned home, he intended on organizing his new steading. Livestock and crops would help provide for his family in Norway and win favorability with his father.

Hallam met him halfway to the church. "Where's your bewitching captive?"

"Hanging from the rafters inside the cottage." There was a measure of amusement in his answer.

"Still refuse to take my advice and sell the she-wolf?"

"I prefer my own plan."

"I'm willing to offer you another path," Hallam said.

A couple of days weren't enough time to judge Silvia. She might prove to be a valuable asset. "Different from before?"

"Four Danes favor an auction."

She was still the talk of the barracks. What did they see in her? Konal shook his head. *A stupid question.* "There's no slave market in *Jorvik*."

"If carried out in secret..."

Why couldn't his kinsman find another vice? "Walk with me." There was only one way to put an end to this growing obsession Hallam and his friends had with Silvia—confront them.

SILVIA FELT NOTHING of her father's presence today. She prayed his spirit would linger for a while longer, but as she looked at his favorite chair, his shelves, and the alcove above the hearth where he kept his treasures, she felt nothing but emptiness. Tears streamed down her face. Curse the Vikings for returning.

But she'd take what blessings she got. Konal was gone for the day, leaving her enough time to do what she needed.

She rushed to the corner by the fireplace where Konal had left his bag. Anger quickly replaced her sadness as she flung it on the table. If he could invade her life, she'd do the same. She untied the satchel and thrust her hand inside. Clothing. Three shirts and a pair of leather breeches that smelled familiar. Like him. At the bottom she found two wood boxes. The first contained a finely crafted necklace of silver and amber beads. The second, a matching ring.

Gifts for his sister? His wife or mistress? The idea of him having someone he loved waiting in Norway should have made her happy. It almost guaranteed that he'd have no long term interest in her. But the thought didn't please her. It hurt knowing she'd be considered little more than an amusement to keep his bed warm for the duration of his stay. *Miserable cur.* She dropped the boxes back in the bag and then stuffed his clothes on top.

Now, she hoped more fervently than ever that she'd be able to retrieve her father's scrolls, give them to a priest for safekeeping, and then return home so she could die in peace. She retrieved her cloak from abovestairs, then went outside. Although spring had arrived, some days were still cold enough to require an extra layer of clothing.

By the time she reached the church, the sun sat in the middle of the sky. The midday meal meant she'd likely succeed because the Danes never missed an opportunity to eat or drink. It grieved her to pass by the skeleton remains of the scriptorium, still smoldering, and the stench of burnt wood filled her nostrils. Would the north ever recover? Ever rebuild? She walked cautiously to the old graveyard, remembering the exact location of the mound. *Bless the soul whose body was meant for this tomb.* She knelt and then started brushing soil away with both hands. She found her other cloak. *Praise God.* Then she dusted it off and peeked inside. *Safe.*

Before heading to the sanctuary, she wandered the grounds, hiding behind trees and outbuildings when a Dane passed by. Where were all the priests? None had been executed. Perhaps Prince Ivarr imprisoned them or they were sequestered inside the church. As a child, she explored freely, often spending the day with one of the monks working outside or in the great kitchen. Men of God liked to eat. And that's where she'd learned to cook.

Facing her home under these circumstances couldn't rob her of the happy memories she had. Father Andrew and Father James were her favorite companions. Both were now elderly men, but as sharp minded and kind as ever. They'd protect whatever precious manuscripts her father chose to preserve.

A *THRALL* REFILLED Konal's cup and then he sucked down his fifth portion of mead. Seated at Ivarr's table, he searched the lower ranks for the men Hallam told him about. He spotted Ulf and Berde sitting with his cousin. *They were no better than hounds begging for scraps.* The sooner he reached his steading, the better.

"When do you leave?" Ivarr queried.

"Tomorrow, milord."

"What delayed your departure?" The prince looked him over. "Have you bedded the wilding yet?"

Konal gritted his teeth. "There's no short answer—I refuse to force myself on her."

"I knew the moment I laid eyes on her what you'd do. That's why I let you keep her."

Konal snorted. "Either I'm too predictable or you can read my mind."

"I recognize the look of a satisfied man." Ivarr shoveled a spoonful of meat into his mouth. "And at this moment, you aren't one, my friend."

"There's no pleasure in rape. I'd have her come to me willingly."

"You admire her?"

Konal wished the subject had never come up. "Aye."

"She's the center of attention around the evening fire. Some call her a Valkyrie. Others suggest she'll kill you before you have a chance to bed her properly. I'm concerned. Do you need some help?" the prince mused.

"He'd rather shovel shite." The rude comment came from below.

Within seconds, Konal was standing with his hand braced on his sword. He glared at Ulf. The bastard had no right to interrupt a private conversation. "I'd sooner disembowel you."

"Is that a formal offer?" Ulf shot back. "The winner takes the whore to bed."

"Konal." The prince rested his hand on Konal's arm. "Leave him, he's not worth it."

He couldn't overlook the insult. Whatever rumors were circulating about *why* he chose to treat Silvia with care, he'd not be mocked for it. Never judge a man for what he did or didn't do in his bedchamber.

The trestle tables were arranged in a rectangle, leaving open space in the middle. Konal stepped off the dais and then kicked the nearest one aside. "Shall I shut your mouth for you?" he taunted. "Let me show you how skilled I am. Bend over and I'll shove my sword up your fucking arse."

Konal. Konal. Konal. Although he was from Norway, he'd won the respect of the Danes.

Ulf nodded his acceptance. He drained his cup and then met Konal between the tables. "To death?"

"To death," Konal agreed.

As was the tradition, both men waited for the prince's approval.

"Is there no other way to settle this dispute?" Ivarr asked.

"Greed corrupts a man," Konal replied. "But envy destroys him. If I leave this bastard alive, milord, I think he'll murder me in my sleep."

"And you?" The prince frowned at Ulf.

"Let the gods pick their victor."

"Prepare to die," Konal warned.

"If you believe that," Ulf said, "you're a bigger fool than I ever imagined."

The murderous look in Ulf's eyes made Konal laugh. He straightened his spine, holding his sword at the ready. His opponent spat and then the tip of his blade slashed through the hem of Konal's tunic. He jumped back, barely avoiding a deeper gash. The man was ready to fight.

Konal cursed and dodged a second strike, edging sideways. Both had something to prove, but his rival overindulged in drink and women too often. That made Konal a better fighter. When their swords met again, the room echoed with the clang.

Konal circled and thrust. Then Ulf charged, but Konal held his ground, landing a powerful blow. The blade bit into Ulf's shoulder. And before he recovered, Konal shifted his hold on his weapon, bringing the blade down on his rival's collar bone. The

Dane howled like a maimed animal.

"Surrender, Ulf." He'd give him one chance to yield and live.

"Aren't you man enough to kill me, Norseman?" Blood stained his arm and chest.

Konal deafened himself to the sounds around him. He'd made a grave mistake attempting mercy for the sake of Prince Ivarr. There'd be no known cowards in his family. And no chance for the bewitching Silvia to question his honor.

Ulf staggered back a few feet, weak from blood loss, then dropped his sword.

Konal didn't want an advantage over his opponent. He, too, laid his sword aside and then drew a knife from his belt.

Someone tossed a short pike to Ulf, and he fell on it, rolling over with it in his hands. The crowd hissed with disapproval.

"Stand if you can," Konal challenged.

He managed to sit, but his face flushed yellow. Judging by the pool of blood he now sat in, Konal knew his death imminent.

"The gods have spoken." Konal sheathed his knife. A lifetime of battles had taught Konal to let a man die where he fell. Even if he was a liar. He faced Ivarr. "I've sworn no oath to withhold my vengeance against these men," he said, gesturing at the throng of bloodthirsty onlookers. "Only to fight for and protect you, milord. I've fulfilled my obligation. This man insulted my honor. As punishment for his insolence, I ask for his head."

"His head?" Ivarr leaned forward.

Ulf moaned and Konal twisted around. "From where I stand, he doesn't require it any longer."

The crowd cheered.

"Jarl Konal the Red," the prince called.

Jarl? No one had ever referred to him that way. He gazed at Ivarr.

"You remind me of our tribal ancestors who once lived in fur shelters and ate each other's flesh to survive harsh winters. Has Odin driven you mad?"

Konal looked down. His armor was covered in blood and he did feel unusually violent. He eyeballed Ivarr and shrugged. "I have my reasons."

"Who am I to deprive you of your trophy?" Ivarr sighed. "Wolves tear their prey to pieces, why shouldn't you?"

Konal didn't want the bastard's head for a prize. He'd deliver it to the Saxon witch who questioned and resisted his every command.

Sunset was still hours off. By Thor, he'd get his reward tonight. "I am, once again, indebted to you, milord."

Konal approached Ulf's body and then reached for the axe slung across his back. "If any of you called him friend and wish to avenge him, step forward now." No one moved. Thankful for the gods' generosity, he raised his weapon. "For Allfather..."

Chapter Seven

DID SILVIA HAVE the courage necessary to defy her captor, to see her father's last wish fulfilled? By sneaking inside the sanctuary, did she risk the lives of the men who'd protected her growing up? Her answer came in the form of a bone-crushing hug Father Andrew gave her the moment she found him praying in the vestry.

"My child..."

Her heart beat so fast she felt dizzy. "Father Andrew, how can I bear it? My sire gone." She collapsed against his shoulder. Until now, she'd held in her pain. "All that's left are these." She offered her cloak.

He ignored it and cupped her chin the same way he always had whenever she cried as a child. "God's will."

She sniffed, unable to accept the idea that *any* god would send a plague as gruesome as a Danish army to slaughter the faithful. "No matter what you say, I cannot believe the Almighty would do this." She'd been surrounded by the bodies of dead men. How did that glorify God?

"Remember the Israelites as Moses led them from captivity in Egypt?" he asked.

She nodded.

"How quickly did they forget God's mercy and turn to idolatry and fornication? We, too, have failed somewhere along the way. We cannot question the Lord's will. Nor can we doubt it and hope to receive His favor."

"But my father remained one of the most pious men I've ever known. If it wasn't for me, he would have taken vows, joined you in service."

"Aye," Andrew whispered. "And would have been a welcome addition. But he loved you more."

She felt responsible for his death. If she'd never been born, perhaps her sire would have been somewhere else during the raid. Spared. Out of respect for the elder, she kept her lingering doubts to herself. "My father directed me to save these manuscripts." She unfolded the cloak, revealing the scrolls.

The monk rubbed his nose. "Did you look at these my child?"

"No," she said. "I wouldn't betray my father's trust."

He accepted the bundle. "There's nowhere safe to hide them, not even here." His gaze swept the alcove. "Ivarr sent a list of demands to Father Joshua this morning. The sanctuary, even our quarters are to be searched. This uprising has set us back a century. Aelle acted before he considered the consequences." He sighed. "And look where he is now."

His mutilated carcass was nailed to a post beyond the courtyard to serve as a deterrent for anyone else tempted to lead a rebellion.

"Prince Ivarr has gone as far as to forbid more than two Saxons to meet in the public thoroughfare. Until we've regained his favor, everyone is under suspicion. Men, women, and children alike."

Any freedoms they'd enjoyed since the Danes first invaded were now gone. So much for faith. So much for tolerance. "What are you saying?"

"The best thing you can do, my child, is leave York. Take

these books with you." He offered them back.

"You haven't learned of my fate yet." She stared at the stone floor, ashamed. "I've been claimed by a Norwegian captain under Prince Ivarr's command."

He coughed, then grasped her arm. "Did he…"

"No," she answered, looking up. "I told him I'd rather die."

The priest's cheeks turned red. "These heathens are an abomination—Cain's offspring—scattered to the four corners of the earth after God cursed his murdering soul."

"No matter who their forefather is," she observed, "I'm afraid my fate is sealed. These blessed texts will be no safer with me. Please," she pleaded, "keep them."

He refused, pushing the books into her hands. "Sometimes blessings come from what appear to be misfortunes. Keep these, Silvia. Hide them amongst your personal effects. Don't read them until the Lord has revealed the appropriate time. Swear on everything holy, promise me you'll abide by what I say." The monk's green eyes widened.

She felt a prick of fear. "I swear."

"There's still time for me to take your confession."

She hugged the scrolls to her chest. Confession? In the middle of a bloody war? Not a physical battle, but the one raging inside her heart. Hatred and doubt—dark thoughts of death. How could she declare these sins?

"Kneel, child."

Reluctant to do so, she slowly prostrated herself. "What do you want me to say, Father?"

He stared down at her. "Your heart is burdened. Don't fear God's retribution."

"When the beast kissed me, I felt something…" she blurted.

Father Andrew rested his chin on his fist. "Continue."

"A sensation I've never known. And then I kicked him between the legs—wishing him dead. Begging to take my own life."

"All perfectly natural reactions to the shock you've suffered."

"Priest," a voice echoed from somewhere in the nave.

"Ivarr's men." He held his finger to his mouth. "You must follow the hallway to the cloister and exit through the back door. Do not stop for anyone. Go." He helped her climb to her feet. "Remember what I told you. God does not abandon the innocent."

Silvia started for the heavy, wood door that opened into the corridor. She'd snuck into the monastery many times as a girl, only to be greeted by the men who'd grown to love her as a favorite pet. They'd gone as far as to feed her sweet bread and warm milk before they pretended to chastise her and sent her home.

"Father?" she called over her shoulder.

Andrew smiled.

"I'll never forget you."

"Aye," he said. "Go with God."

KONAL TRUDGED TOWARD the cottage, carrying the coarse bag containing Ulf's severed head. The bloodthirsty wench would get her payment. And he'd collect his. He'd gone too long and come too far to let her win. He kicked the door open and then walked to the hearth. He dropped the sack on the table, knocking mud off his boots. He'd drank too much ale—eaten too much meat—and killed a man because that man coveted the woman he hadn't bedded yet.

"Silvia," he yelled, staring at the stairs.

"Milord?"

"Come and see what I've brought you from Prince Ivarr's feast."

Her door creaked open. "I'm not hungry."

"Do you think I brought you scraps from his table?"

"I care little for anything you have to offer."

"Downstairs. *Now.*"

She didn't come quietly, her slippered feet echoing nearly as loud as his boots on the hard floor. "Why have you summoned me?" She gasped at the bloodstained bag. "What have you done?"

Konal plopped down in the nearest chair and then propped his feet on the table. "The proof you demanded." He gestured toward the sack.

She covered her mouth with both hands, her eyes wide with disbelief.

"You dare retreat after everything I went through to find the man who murdered your sire?"

"This proves nothing," she hissed. "Tis likely a Saxon head disguised as a Dane."

"I told you before," he said through clenched teeth. "Do not insult me."

"I speak only truth—if you are so easily offended by it…"

"Open it."

"No." She folded her arms over her center.

"Now."

She fingered the top of the bag then peeked inside. She stumbled back from the table. "My God." She glared at him. "You killed one of your own just to prove your innocence? To earn the right to bed me?"

Konal came at her, but she darted under his arm, running to the opposite side of the table. They stared each other down. He pretended to lunge and she flinched. "You make this harder than it needs to be. I prefer a willing partner in my bed."

"I hear sheep are overly submissive, milord. Perhaps I can fetch one from the shearing shed for you."

"Someday you're going to have to make a choice, Silvia."

She frowned. "I already have."

"The wrong one."

She shook her head. "I have faith in my ability to make the right decisions. My father taught me well."

He believed her. The wench undeniably had proven herself quick witted and determined. If she'd only surrender, he'd be kind. Giving pleasure almost satisfied him as much as receiving it. He stared at her throat. The idea of showering her with kisses whilst she squirmed underneath the weight of his body pleased him.

Circling the table, he caught her by the wrist. He yanked her so hard toward the stairs she stumbled.

"Leave me alone."

He didn't want to pity her, but something about her sad eyes stopped him. "We made a bargain."

"Under duress."

"No one forced you to challenge me."

"No?" She stared up at him as if he'd lost his mind. "How can a man like you understand anything? I'd rather die than bed you." She dropped to her knees, tears streaming down her face. "Nothing you say or do will change my mind."

He opened then closed his mouth. Unknown forces moved inside him. He let go of her wrist, gripping her by the shoulders, instead. Everything she said cut through him like a dull blade leaving his insides mangled. "Curse you, woman." He gave her a rough shake.

Looking away, she wiped a stray tear from the corner of her eye. "What sort of man are you?"

The question caught him off guard. Did he even know the answer? The sort who takes what he wants. At least before he left Norway. Now ... he sighed. Releasing her, he moved two stairs above her. "Get off your knees."

Silvia slowly repositioned herself. She now sat on the lowest step with her back toward him. Neither spoke or moved for several moments.

"This can't go on forever," he said.

"I know."

"You belong to me."

"I belong to God."

"Your god is a coward."

She exhaled loudly. "Why keep me? I'll *never* obey you." She turned sideways, leaning against the wall.

Konal wrestled to keep his feelings under control. "If you refuse to submit, I'll beat you senseless. Remember what I told you before? Don't move unless I give you permission. Don't think without my approval. Nothing has changed," he growled. "Be grateful for what patience I've shown you."

"Grateful?" She pushed a loose strand of hair aside. "For what? The thrashing? Stolen kisses. Or the humiliation I suffered in front of Prince Ivarr and your kinsman?" She raised her chin.

He slapped his hands on his thighs. "Be silent."

"I hate you."

Did she know the destructive power of hate? Realize how quickly it would consume her soul? "I don't think you do." Leaning forward, he grazed her cheek with the back of his hand. Perhaps she required a gentler approach.

"Don't." She jerked away, turning so she could see him.

"Silvia—" He squeezed her cheeks between his thumb and fingers. "Weigh carefully what you say next." Defiance glittered in those solemn eyes. And for a fleeting moment, he considered setting her free. The wench wasn't worth the trouble. But pride ruled Konal's heart. Failure wasn't an option. He'd tame this wilding if it was the last thing he ever did. "We leave tonight."

Perhaps he should sell her. Better to sleep peacefully than worry if she'd slit his throat in the middle of the night.

With a sigh he stood, the anguish on her face not escaping his attention. "For tonight," he observed, "your maidenhead is safe." More undeserved consideration for a thankless girl.

"If we leave, I won't get the chance to make sure my father gets a Christian burial."

"It's a waste of time."

She glared up at him.

He studied her thoughtfully. From the thick lashes framing her almond-shaped eyes to her slim ankles. Nothing displeased him. Not even her sharp tongue. That could be dealt with. What he couldn't ignore was the sheer revulsion she'd shown whenever he touched her. He recognized that hollow look. Bitterness. "The wood and paper inside the scriptorium fueled a fire so hot none of the bodies were recovered."

She laughed. "Don't lie, milord. I know your prince buried them in a mass grave."

He looked at her coldly. "Nothing satisfies you." Before he did something he'd regret, Konal stepped around her, leaving her on the landing.

SILVIA BURIED HER face in her hands. Konal didn't deny her accusation. Her beloved father had been thrown in a hole on unconsecrated ground. What afterlife awaited him? Endless wandering on the outskirts of Heaven and Hades, unworthy of either place? Dwelling on thoughts that did nothing but torment her, would not change her situation. But the memories were still too fresh to forget. After her sire thrust those scrolls into her arms, gasping for shallow breaths, she should have dragged him to the passage—braved the smoke and fire—attempted some sort of escape. A shiver went through her body as new tears blinded her.

After several moments, she climbed to her feet and wobbled abovestairs. The few dresses she owned were sprawled across her bed, her slippers already packed. Feeling her throat constrict, she collapsed on her destroyed mattress. The sobs came in long, violent waves. *Why has God forsaken us?* She rolled onto her side, staring at the ceiling. Father Andrew told her with unmitigated confidence that God does not abandon the innocent. *No*, she thought, *He just lets them suffer and die.*

Sorrow uncoiled inside her stomach and she cried out again, unashamed of her sorrow. She tucked her knees under her chin. Nothing could have prepared her for this. Even her chest ached. "I want my father." There must be something she could do to find relief.

Before she had a chance to decide, the door opened. *No. Please don't come in.* Her bedchamber remained her only sanctuary, the one place she could seek shelter from the Danes. She closed her eyes, pretending she didn't hear Konal.

"*Valkyries ikke gråte, slåss de.*" His voice was deep and comforting.

What did he mean by Valkyries don't weep, they fight? Konal swept her off the bed, cradling her. When she looked at him, his eyes reflected her own sadness. This wasn't the same man who abandoned her on the stairs a few minutes ago. Too exhausted to care, her head rolled against his chest.

"*La meg trøste deg, vise deg en side som du ikke visste eksisterte. Jeg føler din smerte. Har mistet kjære kan tider. Tårer er den samme i alle språk.*"

She didn't want to find comfort in his arms.

He whisked across the room, then settled in the same chair he'd thrashed her on yesterday. His big, warm hands began messaging her all over. Reminding her just where and with whom she kept company. And though she despised him, the more Konal caressed her, the harder it was to hate him.

Chapter Eight

AN HOUR LATER, still entombed in his arms, Silvia raised her head. Konal hadn't moved from the chair—he didn't want to. Providing what relief she needed seemed the natural thing to do. Too often, he'd heard the weeping and gnashing of teeth after battle. Viewed the wives and children, mothers and fathers of the slain from a distance, fortifying his heart so their suffering didn't affect him.

No longer.

His gaze drifted from the window to her face. Her slender fingers were fanned across his chest. For whatever reason she chose to stay, he didn't fully comprehend. Grief crippled the greatest of warriors. A woman's heart, no matter how bent on vengeance, couldn't withstand the same beating as a man's. And tears sounded the same in any language.

When he'd heard her sobs, his heart bled for her. More than he cared to admit.

Curse his vulnerabilities.

"I am sorry for your loss," he started. "Believe me, if it was up to me, all the unnecessary bloodletting would have been avoided."

She wiped away the last of her tears. "Am I supposed to be grateful?"

"No," he said. "But I speak truthfully. I'm not the sort of

man who favors death over negotiation. Norse blood was spilled, too."

"The incomprehensible cries from those men on the gallows still haunt me." She straightened, still perched on his thighs. "What nightmares await when I close my eyes?"

The dark wisps of hair framing her face reminded him of silk. So strong was his urge to touch one, he had to fist his hand. Her composure would dissolve like honey on his tongue if he touched her intimately. "Time is your only benefactor." He nudged her to her feet. "Distance helps, too."

He found himself constantly struggling to find the right words to say. "When we bid farewell to our loved ones," he added, "tears do nothing to aid them. Celebrate your sire's death. He died protecting what he loved most."

"How do you know what my father loved?"

He stretched his arms wide. "Every space available in this house is packed with papers. As a scholar, he revered wisdom. I cannot think of a more honorable death—surrounded by the things you admire."

"Does that mean you wish to die in a brothel?"

Without exception, her scornful words battered his heart. "There is only one way for a Norseman to die." He refused to discuss it. "The hour grows late." He stood. "Finish your preparations. I expect you to be ready to leave within the hour."

He walked to the door and then turned back. "Somewhere along the road, we'll stop and sacrifice in honor of your father."

"Is blood all you think about?" she asked. "Why not take the severed head you presented me with? Surely your warmongering gods prefer human flesh over some innocent creature's skin."

He laughed, fascinated by her strength and resilience. "Whatever man is fortunate enough to take your virtue," he said. "For his sake and yours, I pray he's deaf."

SILVIA SLAMMED THE door shut behind Konal. His biting speeches were wearing her down, and so were his hands. Between her flashes of grief and outrage, she had begun to see the kind of man Konal truly was. Though she hated him for the sake of her people, he was unlike any other man she'd ever met. A conquering enemy with half a heart and great restraint.

But whenever she felt herself softening, she remembered the beloved priests imprisoned in the church. The torched scriptorium. The violent deaths of her people. How Saxons weren't permitted to meet on the streets. But not by Konal's hands. He'd revealed his feelings, why he preferred negotiation over bloodshed.

Quietly, she shoved her gowns in the leather bag she often used when she traveled with her father. Then, after checking to make sure Konal wasn't at the door, she knelt and removed the scrolls from their hiding place underneath her bed. Still wrapped in her cloak, she fitted them between her clothes, adding scraps of material from her sewing table on top.

On the far wall, sitting on a shelf, she found her jewelry box which contained what little treasures her mother had left her. She opened it, finding an amber and silver bracelet, a matching necklace, and a gold ring she slid onto her right index finger. A gift from her sire and the monks upon reaching her eighteenth year. The plain band glowed against her pale skin. She stared at it, remembering the joyous celebration, only a few months past.

How her father fawned over her, reminding her she could read and write better than most men, cook and sew, but how no man in York showed any interest in her. Her father teased her often about it. *Too intelligent and beautiful for them*, he said, *only a prince is worthy of my daughter.*

She'd wear the ring with pride.

Draping the heavy bag over her shoulder, her gaze swept the tiny room a last time. Something deep inside told her she'd never see this place again. All the better, for even her father's spirit had fled their home, the happy memories made here forever destroyed.

She admired the tapestry of the Holy Mother tacked on the wall above the table, the place she'd spent much of her time reading, praying, and dreaming of her future. Now, she felt as if her soul was being suffocated. New tears threatened to spill, but she swallowed the pain, remembering what Konal had told her. *Valkyries don't weep, they fight.*

Because of that, she'd put aside the idea of killing herself and would willingly leave behind her old life. She shut the door and headed belowstairs, welcomed by a set table. She dropped her bag where she stood and then walked slowly to the kitchen. Konal held a trencher of smoked fish and bread.

"Tis easier to travel on a full stomach," he said, easing by her. "I've packed the rest of the food and some linens. I found herbs and ointments we may have need of. And..." He placed the platter on the table. "A pair of silver candlesticks."

"You cannot take them." She followed him to the table. "They belong in the sanctuary."

"Aye," he agreed. "Did you steal them?"

"I'm no thief."

"Then I will keep them safe for you." He tore a large chunk of bread off the loaf and sat down. "Where is the coin purse you offered me before?"

Had she given him too much credit? Would the man take everything? "Tucked away in a place no one will find it."

"You've no need for money."

"Then let me donate it to the church."

He nearly choked on his wine. "You humor me, woman."

She claimed the chair opposite his, careful not to look at him as she helped herself to the much needed repast. Why did he want her money? Surely a man of his rank and success already possessed great wealth.

"The coin," he reminded.

"You'd take everything I have left in the world?"

A smile twitched at his lips. "Only for safekeeping," he said. "From what I remember, you have enough silver to buy passage on any ship. I prefer you to stay where I can protect you."

Or to take advantage of her. "Since you leave me no choice, I will fetch the money for you, milord." She obediently hurried to her bag, hoping he wouldn't look inside it and discover the scrolls.

Surrendering her money meant sacrificing her last chance of freedom, but she remembered why she'd chosen to cooperate. The Lord had protected her for a reason and delivered her into the care of a man with a conscience. Though her father's death justified her doubt in God's mercy, she'd wait to see what her future held.

"Here."

Konal's fingers lingered on her hand too long. "I'm pleased you've decided to obey me instead of fighting."

"If I remain submissive, will you promise never to force me into your bed?" The one thing she'd always resist.

He smiled arrogantly. "Did you forget how I held you in my arms?"

"Providing comfort to a grieving daughter cannot be misconstrued as attraction."

"In time, you'll think differently." He ran his fingers up her arm. "Whatever inspired you to sit on my lap doesn't matter."

He tilted her chin. "Did you forget what I gave you this morning?"

The severed head … she'd forgotten about it. "Is it truly the man who killed my sire?"

"Does it matter?"

"Aye."

"No," he admitted. "But the bastard threatened to harm you."

For a fleeting moment she'd hoped Konal had avenged her father. But how could he know—with the smoke and fire—and the Saxons fighting for their freedom… "Did you kill him?"

"No." he said. "My sword struck no one in the scriptorium. I reserve my skills for the battleground, not for men who bury their faces in manuscripts and wear women's clothes."

"Robes," she corrected.

"Call their garments what you will." He shrugged. "The White Christ surrounds himself with weaklings."

"My God is no coward."

He cupped her face. "Your indomitable spirit alone makes me think twice about him. But beyond you, I've seen no proof of his strength. Odin and Thor deserve my devotion. And I would die defending them. But your holy men flee like scared children instead of fighting."

Savagery pumped hot and fierce through his veins like blood. And there was nothing to say in defense of the priests, for Jesus commanded them to turn the other cheek. And to a man as brutal as Konal, that meant one thing—cowardice.

Chapter Nine

KONAL USHERED SILVIA outside, there'd be plenty of time to debate about her god on the road. First, he needed to bid farewell to Ivarr, a man he'd grown fond of but never wanted to see again. Then he'd collect the five warriors pledged to Konal by the prince—additional reward for his service. Although Konal had gained wealth and a title, he wanted to go home. It had been months since he'd seen the ocean. And before he arrived at his new steading, he planned to ride to the fishing village of Filey, where he could stand atop the vast, red cliffs and gaze across the North Sea.

Three horses were tethered to the trees near a storage shed by the church. He inspected them again; checking the saddles, making sure the horse carrying the supplies wasn't overloaded. He patted the gray beast affectionately, scratching him behind the ear. "You must make an important decision," he told Silvia. "Ride alone or with me."

Sunlight reflected in her eyes like tiny flames. "Alone," she answered warily, gazing at the beasts.

"In so choosing," he said, taking a piece of rope off his weapon belt, "I'm forced to bind your hands."

She stepped back a few feet. "I promise I won't try to escape."

He wanted to believe her. Despite his growing infatuation,

he needed to remember she was a slave. *Thralls* would say anything to get what they wanted. "It's for my protection *and* yours."

"No."

"Silvia. Don't make this harder than it needs to be. Hold up your hands."

She refused.

He raked his hand through his hair. "The time for defiance is over. There is no shame in accepting what you are. But you'll feel the sting of humiliation if you continue to fight me."

Likely realizing her continued resistance was futile, she gave up and offered her wrists. Konal wrapped the rope around them several times and knotted it in the middle. "What happened to the girl willing to do whatever she was told?"

"I am still here, milord."

"Good." He lifted her onto one of the horses. "I give you fair warning. Keep a civil tongue when you meet any Danes. Or say nothing at all. Few would endure your bitter tongue."

She swallowed, visibly concerned. "What you shared earlier about the man you killed..."

"Aye," he said. "Several have expressed interest in you."

She lowered her head—ashamed by the idea of so many men noticing her. She'd always been chaste, not the kind of girl to draw attention to herself.

"Don't worry, Silvia. As long as you are with me, none will harm you. Now hold on to the saddle, I'll lead you through the city."

"Please," she begged, her gaze darting about the yard. "Don't take me—I'm of no use to you. Let me stay in the place I love."

"Death sits on every man's shoulder on this island—Saxon and Dane alike. How long do you think it will be before more ships arrive and strip your precious churches of their wealth and rape your women? How long do you think you'd survive?"

Instead of pressing her for an answer, he mounted his steed, leaving her to consider his words. They turned north beyond the courtyard, rounding the crowd of people visiting the armory and food stands. Konal sniffed the air and frowned. Only in Saxon cities did he find the appealing smell of fresh bread mingled with the stench of shite.

Thatched-roofed cottages lined the narrow road and children played wherever they could. Konal navigated carefully to keep the horses from trampling anyone. After a few blocks, he turned in the saddle to check on Silvia. She sat as straight and proud as a captive princess.

Satisfied, he faced forward again and crossed under a stone archway. As if they entered another world, the grunts, curses, and sounds of battle greeted him. The open space was used for training. He slid off his horse, searching the enclosed yard for Ivarr. The two-story stone house in the background served as officer's barracks.

"Come to gloat?" A dark-haired Dane strutted over, sword in hand.

Konal smirked, grasping his arm in friendship. "To collect you and the other men the prince promised me."

"And perhaps to unload your precious cargo?" His gaze traveled slowly over Silvia.

"Pick another field to plow. The girl stays with me for now," Konal said. He glanced at her, then stroked her leg, hoping for a smile. "Meet Jahn."

"Sir—"

"Forgive her curtness." Konal cut her off. "I've given her every reason to be unhappy."

"Aye," Jahn acknowledged with a wide grin. "The bastard

has a habit of disappointing women."

"Don't be so critical," Konal said, "or the girl will never accept me." Konal tapped Silvia's leg. "Time to come down." He reached for her. "The prince wishes to make his goodbyes—he'll want to see you, too."

"Like this?" She held up her hands, still ashamed.

"No one will be looking at your hands," Jahn assured her.

Konal disliked what he was implying, but he couldn't fault a man for admiring his little captive. Silvia slid into his arms and shivered.

"I'll stay with you," he said as he set her on her feet.

They entered the great hall in silence. Ivarr's standards covered the walls, leaving no trace of the Saxon earl who once lived there. Half a dozen trestle tables arranged in the center of the room were filled with men. All conversation stopped when Konal approached the dais where the prince sat.

"Tis good to see you again my friend," Ivarr greeted. "I'm pleased to know you survived another night with the vixen."

The ensuing laughter from the crowd did little to help Silvia relax. Konal gave her a testy look, then bent his head in recognition of the prince. "We've reached an agreement, milord."

Ivarr eyed her hands. "One that involves a bit of rope."

"I prefer her sharp tongue over a blade."

"Small mercies." The prince's gaze was keenly focused on Silvia. "Are you distressed over leaving your home?"

She tried to hide her shaky hands under her cloak. Konal draped his arm across her shoulders. "Don't be afraid to speak," he whispered. "Ivarr does you a great honor by addressing you directly." He nodded toward the prince.

"It grieves me deeply," she answered.

Ivarr stood. "You have my sympathies. This great city has

suffered immensely. But if your brethren will once again trust me, I promise to rebuild it."

Konal didn't know what to think. Rarely did his former commander recognize a Saxon as anything more than dust beneath his feet.

"I've learned of your father's death." Ivarr stepped off the dais, limping and carrying a wood box. "Scholars are valuable, even to a heathen like me. As you know, my interests extend beyond trading and the agricultural value of these lands. Had I known your sire was inside the scriptorium, I would have protected him."

She shifted on her feet, staring at the floor. "Your consideration is appreciated, milord." She raised her head.

Konal could feel the tension creeping up her spine.

"I know reparations cannot restore your happiness." The prince stood in front of them now. "But in my country, when someone is killed—accidently or otherwise—it is customary to offer *wergild* to the surviving family members. In this case, I wish to give you this." He opened the box.

Embroidered gowns and jewels. Konal licked his lips. "Thank you." He spoke on her behalf.

"Let her speak freely," Ivarr commanded.

Although her hands were bound, Silvia ran her fingers over the light-colored fabrics. Then, she picked up a silver collar embellished with sapphires.

"A necklace fit for a jarl's wife," the prince said.

"Milord," she said. "These gifts are too rich for the daughter of a scribe. What shall I do with them?"

Ivarr smiled. "Whatever you see fit."

She curtsied.

"As for your escort." Ivarr turned his attention to Konal. "I'm willing to promote you and offer more gold if you'll stay another year. Few men accomplish what you have in such a short time. Half my warriors love you, the others want to stick a knife in your back."

Konal laughed. He'd already demonstrated what he'd do to any man who challenged him. "Your praise is gift enough, milord."

"Ah," Ivarr said. "I know there's nothing I can do to keep you here. Your father's ship arrived a week ago. His men will meet you soon. Go with the gods, Jarl Konal." He thrust the box in Konal's hands.

Konal hesitated for a moment. He'd made a name for himself here, established friendships, fought in one of the bloodiest sieges and survived. With gold and silver and other assets at his disposal, he'd return to Norway a respected man. But as the second in line for his father's seat of power, what really awaited him across the sea? For he could never accept his eldest brother's rule after tasting what it felt like to be a jarl. If he stayed, there were no limits. But his heart ached for the icy blue fjords and mountains, the forest and snow, and family.

Ready to go, he grasped Ivarr's arm with his free hand. *"En medvind på ryggen vår er best."* A fair wind at your back is best.

Chapter Ten

"IS IT SO bad keeping company with me?" Konal stared down at Silvia from his horse with an unreadable expression. "The evening sky is clear. And the winds are light. We'll sleep comfortably tonight without a fire."

Only if she could get him to free her hands and stay as far away as possible. After half a night and a full day of riding, her arse ached. Twenty miles into their journey, she no longer recognized the countryside. Having only traveled a few miles beyond York, her whole life revolved around the familiar sights and sounds within the city walls. And the cottage. The further away she got, the heavier her heart grew. She prayed silently, remembering her father and the men who died trying to reclaim the city. She begged for guidance, patience, understanding, and even a bit of forgiveness for the man who continued to protect her from the savages that surrounded them.

The five soldiers escorting them were little better than ravenous dogs. Dressed in full armor, thick beards braided and adorned with silver and gold beads, they reminded her of everything she feared. Heathens with little else to do but search for something to kill. Three of them went hunting the minute Konal picked a place to camp for the night. The other two wandered off to piss—an announcement she wished she'd never heard.

As she surveyed the area, she admired the creek that cut through the flatlands, disappearing into the forest. Fields of wheat and barley dominated the eastern landscape. Bleating sheep could be heard from a nearby farm.

Dismounting, Konal untied her hands. "We're far enough away from Jorvik to trust you again."

She rubbed her sore wrists, unhappy with the marks left by the rope. "You think me incapable of finding my way home?"

"No," he said. "I think you're too shrewd to make the mistake of walking alone. And..." He seized her right wrist. "There's nothing left for you there."

He couldn't be more wrong. Perhaps he didn't understand how closely connected she was to the monks. It might seem improper to some—immoral even—but men of the cloth loved children, too. And no matter how old she grew, those precious servants of God still regarded her as the same little girl running wild inside the sanctuary.

She glared at him, very aware of his touch.

Whenever she looked at Konal, it forced her to remember. "Please don't touch me. I'm a slave now. Assign me a task so I feel useful."

He untied his saddle packs, then threw them on the ground at her feet. "Shake out the furs and make our beds. We'll reach the coast by tomorrow afternoon."

"The coast?" she repeated anxiously.

"Aye," he said. "The North Sea."

"I-I thought we were going to your steading."

His mouth twitched. "We're headed in that general direction," he confirmed. "Once we reach the crossroads, I'll send the guards ahead to warn my tenants of our arrival." He studied her critically. "*We're* going to Filey."

Although she feared the soldiers, their presence made it

difficult for Konal to get her alone. "Why Filey?"

"To see the ocean."

She cared nothing about the coast.

"You've never set eyes on the water, have you?"

"There's been no cause, milord. I've seen my share of rivers and lakes, what need of an ocean?"

His eyes sparkled with amusement. "You know little of the world."

She disagreed. "I know more about the world than most," she challenged. "After the things I've read, the secrets divulged in manuscripts collected from as far as Constantinople, believe me when I say men's hearts are as cold and bent on violence a thousand miles away as they are here."

"A fair argument," he admitted. "But the intentions of men have nothing to do with the wondrous sights beyond this island."

She couldn't understand why anyone would want to leave their home for foreign shores. "My responsibilities kept me close to the church, near my father and the monks. Don't you have a family? A wife and children?"

"The truth is revealed," he said. "Waiting for the right time to ask questions so it doesn't appear you're truly interested in me." He smiled. "I have many brothers and a sister. My father anxiously awaits my return. But a wife…" He shook his head. "I've avoided marriage for a long time."

"Norsemen breed like rabbits to keep their armies stocked with bloodthirsty boys."

A light breeze lifted his dark hair. "Children are a man's future," he said with absolute certainty. "And in time, I'll sire as many as Odin is willing to give me." He fingered his beard. "As for breeding like rabbits, shall we test your theory?"

Silvia fisted her hands at her sides. "You twisted the meaning of my words again."

"Have I now?"

"You'd find any excuse to act churlish."

"According to you," he said, stepping closer. "I don't need one. It's in my tainted blood."

Boiling blood, she thought. Something strange happened between her legs then—a tiny spasm and a surge of wet heat. Embarrassed by whatever she was experiencing, she looked away, only to find herself staring at his full lips a minute later. That mouth had plundered hers, tasted her, and left her mindless. *Stupid girl.* She smoothed her skirt, as nervous as she'd ever been with him.

"How many times have you looked at a man the way you just stared at me?"

"What?"

"Tell me now what you were thinking when you gazed at my mouth."

"You're imagining things, milord."

"Stop denying what you naturally feel, Silvia."

Lord help her. "This is a pointless conversation."

"Is it?"

She tried to grab the bags, but he took her hand, forcing her upright.

"Indulge your master," he said sweetly. "Let's play a game, Silvia."

"I'm not overly fond of such things," she lied. The monks taught her how to play chess before she could speak. And she knew how much Norsemen enjoyed sporting of any kind. Whether *hnefatafl,* a game similar to chess, or drinking in excess.

"Tis a game of wit," he offered. "Or truth, if that's what you choose to call it."

Admittedly, he'd piqued her interest. "What are the rules?"

"I'll ask you a question, and if I think your answer is misleading, I win a kiss."

Her eyes narrowed. "This supposed game seems slanted in your favor."

"On the contrary," he assured her. "You, too, receive the same opportunity."

That made her laugh. "If I think you're withholding the truth I get to kiss you? Hardly a coveted prize for me."

"What does that mean?"

"You've kissed me before, milord. I didn't like it."

Without warning, his lips brushed across hers. She gasped and stepped back. His mouth wreaked havoc on her insides. What chance did she really have against this man? Her gaze slipped down his body, focusing on the calloused hands resting at his sides. It was almost impossible not to think of how it felt to be pawed by them. Every inch of him as virile as a rutting stag.

"Consider this the start of our match," he said. "Tell me exactly what you are thinking."

Confessing would only feed his ego. But he had proven too perceptive already, he'd know if she withheld anything. "Your hands," her voice wavered. "I've never seen a larger pair."

He grinned. "You're not the first woman to accuse me of being large."

She covered her mouth in disgust, fully aware of what he meant. "Men who boast about such things are often said to be liars, milord."

"There's no need for me to lie."

Why should she doubt him? Every other part of his body was oversized. With the exception of his brain. She chuckled.

"What?" he demanded.

"A private thought."

"There can be no secrets between us," he said, holding her gaze. "As a member of my household, I'm entitled to know even the most insignificant thought."

She shook her head. "I believe it's my turn."

"Aye." He brought her hand to his lips and kissed it. "So it is."

"Tell me about your family." If she distracted him with a certain kind of questioning, maybe he wouldn't have time to think about kissing her again.

His head tilted thoughtfully to the side. "Of all the things you could ask, this is what you wish to know?" He rubbed his chin. "My father is named Brandr, my mother was Thordia. We live in the Trondelag, one of Odin's most sacred places. I have three brothers and a sister. My father is proud, a respected *jarl*. My sister, beautiful and obedient."

"Traits I am sure all Northmen cherish."

"Is it so objectionable to do as you're told?"

"Is this your query, milord?"

A crease appeared between his eyebrows. "It seems you've outwitted me this round, Silvia. Yes, answer the question."

"Don't you know the answer? I'm freeborn, the daughter of a scholar. A teacher of the wealthiest sons in Northumbria. You presume to steal my freedom because one day your army marches into York and destroys everything I love." Anger swelled inside her chest. "You can shackle a man's hands and feet, not his heart."

"You forget how much a man of my low breeding enjoys a fiery temper." A shadow fell across his features. "Your resistance is a promise of things to come."

"No, milord," she started. "My defiance is proof of my great dislike for your kind."

"Ask a question."

"If you are the son of a Norwegian *jarl*, why are you serving under a Danish prince?"

"You are much too aware of the political conflicts between our countries. What use does a woman have for such knowledge? Your sire should have spent more time preparing you for marriage."

"You didn't answer my question."

"I lost a drinking wager against my elder brother." He gave her a lazy smile, daring her to respond.

She rolled her eyes. "You seem proud of your loss."

"I'd wear it as badge on my chest if I could." He waved his hands. "I turned that defeat into a victory. Now it is my turn," he informed her. "How many men have you kissed?" He grazed her bottom lip with his knuckles, sending a shockwave of excitement through her.

"Tis an inappropriate question." She crossed her arms over her chest.

"You cannot change the rules because you dislike my inquiry."

She frowned. "None."

He tilted her chin upward, gazing into her eyes. "Do Saxon men prefer boys?"

She clicked her tongue reprovingly. "Our thriving numbers prove otherwise."

"Men wearing dresses—girls in libraries—a beautiful woman never kissed. I'm beginning to suspect the gods opened up your lands to us because of the effeminate nature of your men."

"You went out of turn, milord. Now I get two chances."

He accepted her words, then stepped back, moving with powerful grace, another thing she regretfully admired about him. Large men often stumbled over their own feet. Not Konal.

"How many women have you bedded?"

He nearly choked. "Too many to count."

Ten? Twenty? Thirty? Too many to count? It appalled her, but struck her as an honest reply. She remembered the jewelry in his bag. That wasn't a safe question to ask a man. She tapped her fingers against her mouth.

"I'm waiting, Silvia."

As far as she was concerned, he could wait until the end of bloody time. She didn't like this game.

HE LONGED TO touch her again, only Konal wanted it to be her choice. Another question about his sexual prowess would give him every reason to caress her face. She opened her mouth as if she was determined to say something, but then snapped it shut. By the gods, he wanted to shove something between those sensual lips. "What has silenced you?"

"There is no point to this game."

It had taken her longer than he'd expected for her to realize it. "You are correct."

"A waste of time then," she complained. "Daylight is fading, we must prepare."

He shrugged, unconcerned. "Sometimes other things take precedence."

Her finely-shaped brows jutted.

"Tis better to get acquainted than worry about setting up camp."

Silvia pulled a fur out of one of the bags. "Why disguise a conversation as a game?"

"You've been less than agreeable when I've tried talking to you before. I made it more appealing and you were willing to play."

"I believe you owe me an apology, milord."

"For what?"

"Taking advantage of my innocence."

"Are you calling me a liar, *again*?"

She looked down, grinding the toe of her boot in the dirt. "Not directly."

"You think there's a difference between direct and indirect falsehoods?"

"One is the lesser of two evils."

Woman logic made no sense. "A lie is a lie."

"I agree wholeheartedly, but only wished to see where you stood on the matter."

"Then you admit we're both guilty and now *two* kisses must be exchanged."

Her eyes were as round as a full moon. "Two?"

"Two." He swept her hair aside, gripping her shoulders as he leaned into her.

Her lips parted and their tongues tangled. The lack of companionship over the last few months in the field had left him half-crazed. But his hunger for Silvia—which grew rampantly whenever he touched her, was nearing a level of explosive proportions he'd never known before.

It gave him good reason to stop. But with his shaft pressed against her stomach, lust overrode his control. Paradise awaited him between her thighs. Slim legs he remembered too well from the night he spanked her. He made a wild sound deep in his throat as one of his hands found the generous swell of her breast. Her pebble-hard nipples protruded through the soft material of her dress, which he quickly touched, and Silvia's body constricted with pleasure.

"I'm sorry," he whispered against her cheek, realizing his mistake. If he took his time, she'd learn to trust him, even crave his attention. But his body disagreed. "That's the first kiss," he muttered. "I'll claim the second now, too."

This time his mouth collided violently with hers, his hands wandering across her body, then around her waist where he cupped her backside. His breath caught in his throat at the feel of her firm arse. Locking her against him with one arm, he found the laces on her bodice and quickly untied them. Her gown gaped open, revealing milky white flesh. He tugged gently on her dress until it loosened enough to fall down her shoulders.

Silvia inhaled and closed her eyes, in Konal's estimation, granting him permission to do whatever he pleased. He admired her exposed breasts, caressing them gently while he sucked on a pink nipple. With every squeeze and lick, she sighed, her hands buried in his hair. So now the spirited wench knew his touch produced a kind of pleasure she'd never experienced. And if she let him, he'd teach her how to get more. How to give as much pleasure as she received. A skill she'd value in the future when she sought the protection of another man.

Curse his stupidity for interfering with her work. If he'd allowed her to arrange the furs, there'd be a bloody place to lay her down. With little concern for who might come upon them in the open, he hiked her skirt over her hips. What greeted him made him salivate. "One taste," he murmured, enthralled by the thatch of dark curls between her legs. "Just one."

IF SHE LET him between her thighs she'd burn in Hell forever. As if jolted from a dream, Silvia opened her eyes. "We cannot do this," she said, suddenly aware of her vulnerability.

But instead of stopping, he knelt at her feet, showering her navel with hot kisses.

"Konal," she said shakily. "Did you hear me?" Each kiss chipped away at her already weak resistance. Then she felt the moist warmth of his tongue around her belly button. His massive hands rested on her thighs. Seeing him posed so close to her nether region made her legs quiver. "Please…"

He raised his head. "You didn't dissuade me before," he growled. "Do you know what danger you face allowing a man so close, then robbing him of the pleasure without good cause?"

His fingernails dug into her skin and she acknowledged the rage in his steely blue eyes. "How could I know if I've never done this before?"

His feelings were of no concern now, the sound of raucous laughter carried on the wind signaled the soldiers were close.

"Damn you, woman." He staggered to his feet, then yanked her skirt back down. "Consider this your only warning. Never tempt a man with honey unless you intend to give him the pot."

Feeling sufficiently humiliated, she said, "You're cruel."

"Am I?" His warm breath raised gooseflesh on her neck. "And what do you consider yourself?" He guided her hand between his legs. "Touch me."

She shook her head. "Why do you tease me?"

"The guards are getting closer … do it and I'll leave you alone."

She stared at him disbelievingly. Misery stained his face. Of course her own body felt raw and unsatisfied. But she steeled herself against the temptation standing before her. If that's what it took to make Konal go away, so be it. She cupped his manhood. A devilish smirk spread across his lips. Secretly, Silvia liked what she felt, and knew what to expect before she touched him.

"You've acquired a taste for me."

"No," she denied. "I meant only to prove my point from earlier. Men who brag about their size shouldn't be trusted to tell the truth."

Chapter Eleven

As Konal tossed and turned on his furs, he tried to banish Silvia's last words from his mind. Did she find him inadequately sized? A virgin who'd never been kissed, much less seen a man naked. *No.* She'd intended to plant a seed of doubt in his bedeviled head. The girl knew how to make him suffer. He sighed and closed his eyes.

Hours later, smoke choked him awake. He threw his furs off and scrambled to his knees, surrounded by a raging fire. The air reeked of pitch. Asleep only feet away, Konal screamed for Silvia to awaken.

"Get up!" He grabbed what gear he could save and walked through the flame and smoke meant to claim his life.

Then he rushed to Silvia, lifted her into his arms, and carried her to safer ground. "Stay here," he said, then turned to the nightmare behind them.

The horses were gone, probably scared away by whoever penetrated their camp. Konal cursed himself for sleeping so heavily and for relying on the protection of men he didn't completely trust. Of the five guards, only Jahn had earned his respect on the battlefield. But he was nowhere to be found.

With a full moon overhead and the flames consuming the dry vegetation around him, Konal had no problem identifying the bodies of three of his men. All murdered, throats cut with their swords still sheathed at their hips. Careless bastards. They'd never expected an attack judging by the half-empty wineskins scattered about. Though he never wished this type of death on anyone, had the Danes taken their responsibilities seriously, perhaps they'd still be alive. He rubbed his face with both hands, wondering who dared attack in the middle of the night.

Before he returned to Silvia, he walked the perimeter of the camp, checking for any signs his enemies had left behind. Perhaps he was overthinking things. Raiders were everywhere, desperate Saxons and marauders who preyed upon unsuspecting travelers. But why cover the ground in pitch and set a fire?

His destination wasn't a secret in Jorvik. And as Prince Ivarr had observed, only half his men loved Konal and the rest wished him dead. After he claimed Ulf's head, Konal was sure he'd made new enemies amongst the Danes, too. Then there was the matter of his lovely captive…

Many reasons existed for someone to try and end his life. But tonight the gods had been generous, not only sparing him, but the beautiful Silvia as well.

He found her wrapped in a fur and pacing nervously.

"What evil has befallen us?" she asked, a look of relief on her face as soon as he appeared.

"I don't know," he admitted. "But I have my suspicions. And in time, the guilty will be brought to justice. I swear it."

"You'll find a sympathetic ear with me," she said. "For I've lived my whole life under the threat of danger from the Danes."

"Aye." She never missed an opportunity to lay her grievances at his feet.

"Where are Jahn and the other guards?"

"Three are dead, murdered where they sat."

"Jahn?"

"Missing."

"Dear God."

"There is nothing else to be done until daylight. Sleep, Silvia," he directed her.

Luckily, the wind was blowing the acrid smoke in the opposite direction of where they stood. And by the look of it, the fire would burn out soon.

"How can I close my eyes knowing someone is lurking in the shadows? What if they return for your blood?" she asked.

"And yours." He regretted it as soon as it slipped out of his mouth.

She shivered. "Then give me a knife."

He laughed darkly. "We both remember what happened last time you held a blade in that lovely hand."

"Circumstances have changed."

"Have they?" He edged closer, his baser feelings surfacing again. Battle and death fueled his need for the touch of a woman. Especially this dark-haired beauty.

"I am helpless in this place—without friends or home."

"You are the least helpless female I've ever met, Silvia. For your tongue is as deadly as a double-edged sword in the hands of the most seasoned warrior. How many times have you aimed your fury at me?"

"I-I am truly sorry, milord."

"Are you?"

"Yes."

Suddenly exhausted, he sucked in a ragged breath. "All right." He unsheathed the smallest of his blades and offered it to her. "Sleep with it close. If someone tries to harm you, aim for the ribs or heart. You'll only get one chance, Silvia. Rely upon the element of surprise if you wish to live."

She accepted the weapon. "Thank you for trusting me."

Then she did something he never expected; she stood on her toes and kissed his cheek. "God be with you."

Within the hour, Silvia had fallen asleep under his careful watch.

SILVIA FELT AS if she'd reached some kind of new understanding with Konal last night. Maybe the fear of the moment made her more conciliatory, realizing he was the only thing standing between her and the threat of death. She studied him with great interest as he ate a piece of bread and took a long drink from his wineskin.

"Your eyes betray you once again," he said without looking at her.

More than irritated by the fact he seemed to know everything she did without needing to glance in her direction, she ignored his words. "Good morn." She sat up.

"Four of the horses have returned," he offered. "But no sign of Jahn or Ansgar."

"Will we search for them?"

"No." He stood and stretched. "I followed a trail of blood at sunrise, but it revealed nothing. Our attackers may have taken them prisoner or perhaps we were betrayed."

"Betrayed?" That piqued her interest and she crawled from underneath the warmth of her furs. "Not all men pledge blind allegiance to my master?"

He chuckled, his rugged face dark with several days' worth of stubble. "I ask no one to follow me, Silvia. But if they choose to do so, loyalty is an unspoken expectation. I have cut down dozens of men for swearing falsely in the name of the gods. Dane or Norse, Saxon or otherwise."

She approached him tenuously, still intimidated by his hulking body and the way he stared at her whenever she came near. "I am hungry and thirsty."

He stepped out of her way, revealing a linen that he'd spread on the ground behind him, with a loaf of bread, dried fish, and cheese set out. "Tis not a feast, but it will quiet the rumbling in your gut."

She took the wineskin first and drank until her thirst was quenched. "Do we still ride for the coast?"

"Aye," he said. "I think it better to surprise my new tenants."

Once she finished eating, she packed the food and furs away, then readied herself, combed her hair and put her boots on.

Konal inspected the horses and bags before he turned back to Silvia. "Today, you will ride with me."

She didn't dare protest, and held up her hands, expecting to be bound.

"There is no need," he said. "If we are attacked on the trail, I would have you free and able to fight alongside me."

The prospect of being attacked frightened her severely. Though she'd grown accustomed to violence in her young lifetime, imagining it happening out here in the open, where there was nowhere to run, left her unsettled. But she'd never reveal that fear to Konal. He expected her to remain clear-minded and strong.

He lifted her onto his steed, then mounted behind her. The other horses were tied together and would follow behind.

"See the devastation?" he whispered in her ear. "You, too, were surrounded by flames." He pointed to where her original sleeping spot had been.

The earth was scorched black. She shuddered at the thought of being burned alive—a type of execution reserved for witches. Just above the devastated area, the hillside bloomed with life. Green grass and colorful wildflowers dotted the landscape. Even the sunshine seemed unusually healing this morning, warming her bone deep.

"Thank you again," she said sincerely. "If you hadn't carried me away, I'm afraid I would have died in my sleep."

"Nothing will touch you as long as you stay with me, Silvia." He wrapped one powerful arm about her waist, then gently tapped his heels against the horse's sides. "Barbarian or not, I will protect what is mine to my very last breath."

Did he know how potent his words were? How deeply they affected her? That she was starting to believe in everything he said and did? That she admired him for not being like the other invaders?

She suspected the heart of a true champion existed somewhere beneath his rough exterior. At least she hoped so, because someday in the near future, she would appeal to the gentler side of this warrior and ask for her freedom.

Chapter Twelve

CONCERNED FOR THEIR safety, Konal elected to take a less traveled route to Filey. It meant an extra day of riding through the vale, but it seemed worth it, for any time alone with Silvia would get her closer to his bed. He could see it in her fathomless, blue eyes and in the way she carried herself now. Still cautious, but no longer terrified.

As the sun set, he returned to the camp in the woods with two ducks he'd snared. Eating dried fish and hard bread for more than a couple days did not appeal to him. A hearty fire awaited and Silvia greeted him with a skin filled with water.

"We'll have fresh meat tonight," he said, handing her the birds. "Do you know how to pluck feathers, little *thrall*? Or shall I teach you?"

She sat down on a flat rock near the fire and held one of the birds up by its feet. "Once I finish with this," she said with authority. "You may clip the wings and necks off."

A short time later, Konal chose a couple sturdy tree branches, and with his knife, split them into quarters to construct a spit and skewers. Once both birds were cleaned and cut properly, he shoved a thick branch through each carcass, following the spine, then fit the notched ends of the sticks onto the spit.

"Turn the birds as often as possible so the meat cooks evenly," he advised. "Now if you no longer require my assistance, I am going to take a bath."

"A bath?" She looked about. "Here?"

"In the river." Laughter rumbled in his chest. "Tis only a short distance away, Silvia. If you need me, call my name." The wench had never said it before, only milord and master, or other vulgar words no girl should know. He longed to hear his name slip from her lips—preferably while he pumped inside her.

Standing on the riverbank now, he breathed in the fresh air and appreciated how the frothy water tumbled over the moss-covered boulders. He'd braved the rapids of many waterways in Norway as a boy, learning to swim and control a small boat that way. A rite of passage any boy faced in order to become a man. And if he walked away without broken bones or a crushed skull, all the better.

He stripped, then waded out. Not as frigid as the glacial rivers back home, but very satisfying. Scrubbing his face and body first, he paid careful attention to his underarms and between his legs. Saxons weren't known for their cleanliness and it had taken the Danes a long time to teach them how to build a functional bathhouse. Another reason he longed for home.

Just as he emerged from the depths, he caught a flash of blue fabric from the corner of his eye. He grinned, knowing it was Silvia hiding in the trees. Though she pretended to not be interested in his body, he'd caught her on more than one occasion studying his physique. A natural instinct for any woman her age. But once again, the monks had destroyed what the gods had intended as a gift for all men and women. Lust assured the White Christ's followers a place in Hades.

Just to satisfy her curiosity, he stood up slowly, raking his fingers through his shoulder-length hair. Then he turned around, facing away from her, and bent over, sure his legs were wide apart.

"Good God," he heard from the woods.

"Is something amiss?" he asked, not moving.

"Amiss?" Silvia repeated. "I cannot open my eyes until you come out of the water and dress."

Konal hadn't laughed so hard in a long time. "Why are you here?" He straightened and twisted around, finding her standing in the open, her hands covering her face.

"Looking for herbs and berries."

He tsked as he headed for shore, knowing it was too early in the year for wild berries. "From the moment we met, Silvia, I admired your indomitable spirit and will to survive, even your sharp tongue, but never thought you a liar." He stood in front of her now, unashamed of his nakedness.

Her eyes popped open, her hands fisted at her sides. "I am not a liar."

"No?" he asked, teasing her relentlessly. "What were you going to carry these berries in?" He eyed her head to toe.

She didn't attempt to answer his question.

"Confess, Silvia. You were spying on me."

Her cheeks turned red. "And why should I do that?" Her gaze darted to his manhood, then back to his face.

She'd get no sympathy from him. There was no relief for his own suffering unless she offered her body freely to him. "I desire you more than any woman, Silvia," he said, all humor fading. "I want to kiss you. Touch you. Taste you. Fuck you."

"T-that cannot happen."

"Why?" He stepped closer and she edged back.

"We are not promised in marriage."

"Forget what the priests taught you. Tis only us here, surrounded by nature. Even the beasts enjoy the gift of passion."

"So you admit you are as lowborn as a wild creature? Driven by instinct. Without a heart or conscience."

"I admit that I want you." He cupped her cheek then, liking the heat and softness of her flesh. "And I know you feel the same."

Surprisingly, she didn't reject his touch, only stood there, locked in an endless stare with him.

"The meat will burn if I don't get back to the fire."

"Let it." He cradled her face with his other hand, his heartbeat thundering. "Feed me in a different way, Silvia."

"Why should I trust you?"

"Because there isn't another man in this Odinforsaken country that will treat you as tenderly as I will. Your pleasure is as important to me as my own. I will not fuck you and walk away. When it's time for me to go, I will provide for your future care."

For a brief moment it appeared she was seriously considering his words. For her features softened a bit and her fingers trailed up his arm. "You are a handsome man," she said. "Powerful and fierce, a jarl. And I am your unfortunate slave. That fact will never change. And knowing it breaks my heart. For I am freeborn. A follower of Christ. Not your lover."

She withdrew her hand.

"Then why are you here?"

"I wanted to be near you."

He lowered his head and kissed her softly, then separated from her a little so he could see her face clearly. "There is no reason to hide then." Before she could speak, he kissed her again, finding her pink tongue.

This kind of self-torture didn't suit Konal. He wanted more of her—all of her if she'd just say yes. "Do you feel it?"

"How can I not?" She gasped. "Tis wedged between our bodies."

He meant the mutual attraction. "Aye," he acknowledged his erection. "I cannot hide the truth from you. No man can."

"Does it hurt?"

"Yes, a deep ache."

She turned away. "I will finish preparing our meal."

"Aye," he said, reaching for his tunic on the ground. "Run away, little thrall. Only a woman can handle what I have to offer."

Chapter Thirteen

AS SILVIA CHEWED on the roasted duck, she kept sneaking looks at Konal. He'd returned from the river more silent then he'd ever been with her. Though she usually welcomed the peace, for reasons she didn't know, she craved the familiarity of his rich voice. Regardless of their positions, master and slave, he often made her laugh and forget the pain of the recent days, if only temporarily.

"You are angry at me?" she braved asking.

He didn't look up. "No."

"Do you regret bringing me along?"

"No."

"Will we arrive in Filey tomorrow?"

"By everything sacred..." He tossed a bone in the fire pit. "I thought you didn't like playing the question game."

"I find the silence between us unbearable."

"Perhaps you should have considered the consequences before you invaded my privacy at the river."

"I didn't know you owned the woods and river, milord. I will be sure to ask your permission before I seek ingredients for our meals." Her voice shook as she spoke, but she couldn't allow him to get the best of her. She was quickly learning how to challenge him without sparking his anger.

Though she had specifically ventured to the river to see the flex of his muscles and the way his body would glisten in the fading sunlight when wet—what he didn't know wouldn't hurt him. Like all the things no chaste girl would ever brood about. But Silvia didn't consider herself the same as other women. Her body might be inexperienced, but her mind burned with fantasies. And if she didn't tread carefully around this man, he'd make sure her body caught up with her thoughts.

"You'd be smart to remember not to take a step without my permission," he reminded her.

"Unless my path leads to your bed."

Dark blue eyes met hers. "I've made it clear how your stubbornness arouses me, Silvia. If you continue to provoke me, what makes you think I won't take what I want?"

"I've seen the irreversible damage done by unscrupulous men in York. Rape and violence. Bastard children born to Saxon women whose fathers were nowhere to be found. How can you suggest such a thing, even if those threats are empty?"

"Is that what you think of me?" He shot up, the linen draped across his lap with food on it, fell to the ground. "Am I weak because I haven't claimed you?"

"No," she said. "You are a better man than most."

He paced on his side of the fire.

"I know you had no choice in coming here," she started. "But from everything I've learned, the Danes come to gain wealth and power, or to spill blood. But not you, milord. You show little interest in anything."

He sighed. "In Norway, fertile land is scarce. My family is fortunate to own enough to feed ourselves and the people who serve us. Hundreds have fled our country in search of a new life. And the wars… There is only tentative peace between the Norse and Danes. Men serving under Prince Ivarr have crossed our borders and salted the soils so nothing will grow. Do you know how long it takes for the fields to recover? Men faced with starvation will do anything to fill their hungry bellies."

"Is that what you hoped to gain? Farmable lands?"

His jaw clenched. "My steading here will provide additional crops. I left Norway a second son and return a jarl. That is all you need to know."

"I only wish to understand your motivations, to know you better."

"That is not your concern, Silvia. You will serve me. If I command you to cook my meals or arrange my furs, you will do so without hesitation. My private affairs are my business alone."

"You called out for Eira in your sleep."

He gave her a hard look. "Never speak that name aloud."

She marveled at his sudden turn in mood. Who was Eira, and why did her lovely name inspire such coldness? "Forgive me, milord." She rushed to pick up the food he'd dropped.

After she finished her work, she addressed Konal. "I seek permission to go to sleep, milord."

"Aye," he said. "Keep the knife I gave you close by."

She'd arranged her pallet several yards away from Konal's, out of reach, but close enough to feel safe. Before she faded, she watched him move about the fireside, deeply troubled by something, muttering to himself, and occasionally staring heavenward. No doubt he'd loved this Eira with all his heart. And for the first time in Silvia's life, for the briefest moment, she wished she'd been born someone else.

"I AM NOT a fool," Konal repeated out loud. "Nor a coward or weakling. I don't depend on my sire for sustenance as my brothers do. I don't cling to a wife or serve any man but myself. But I cling to memories. Bitter ones..."

He'd not heard his former lover's name spoken out loud in years. For anyone that knew him dared not say it lest he carved their tongues out.

"I am Konal the Red. Odin is my master. My axe and sword are ready to answer the call for war. I don't fear death. I dream of Valhalla. Women sigh in my presence. Men step aside as I pass by."

All these things he must convince himself were still the truth, for the tiny Saxon asleep on the furs had nearly brought him to his knees. Not because she uttered the name of a woman he once admired and loved, but because she was pure and so unwaveringly brave. He didn't know what to do with her. Silence her forever or keep her at his side. On more than one occasion since they'd met, he thought her a gift from Odin himself. For she saw things with a rare clarity.

The ache between his legs now matched the constant ache in his heart. He walked around the fire and stood over her, watching the rise and fall of her chest as she slept.

The idea of his misery infecting another soul bothered him. He'd not only sworn loyalty to Prince Ivarr before he sailed to Northumbria, he'd also promised to leave his past behind. To make new memories. To return a healed man. But once his resolve was truly tested, he fell apart.

He knelt beside her, caressing her cheek with the back of his hand. "You ask too many questions. Ones I don't want to answer. Tis no fault of yours, sweet Silvia. For three years ago, I was a different man. The kind that would have welcomed your friendship. You'd do best to keep away from me."

As he started to stand, she gripped his wrist and stared up at him, her eyes wide with wonder. "Please," she choked out. "Don't leave."

Tears leaked out of her eyes.

"You don't know what you are saying."

"I recognize pain," she said. "You grieve as I do. I will not ask you any more questions, milord. But I offer what comfort I can in exchange for what relief your warmth and strength can give me. For tonight, I sorely miss my father."

Konal licked his lips. For days he'd fantasized about crawling into her bed. But that's not what she offered him now. This was much more. A show of unmitigated trust.

"Sometimes, I think the men who die are fortunate," he said. "For this world is cruel and unpredictable. One day we live in peace, the next we are plunged into war. Mourn your father, girl, but don't begrudge him his eternal rest, for whatever place he ended up in, is surely better than this."

Agony overwhelmed him. Curse his weakness.

She pulled the furs back. "Will you join me?" She rolled onto her side, facing away from him, the invitation left open.

He admired the curve of her back, the appeal of her tiny body waiting for his to curl up next to her. *Yes*. He'd risk it, and slid underneath the furs and tugged her into his arms.

Warmth and soft flesh greeted him. He buried his face in her long, fragrant hair, breathing in her feminine scent. She was everything he'd hoped for, her closeness a peace blessing upon his soul.

"Are you comfortable?" he finally spoke.

"I am aware."

A strange thing to say. "Of what?"

"Everything," she whispered. "I can hear my own heart-beat."

Then he understood. She'd never lain in the arms of a man. And from his own experience, the first time he shared a bed with a woman, his senses were intensified by a hundredfold.

"You have restored my peace," he said, stroking her back.

And resurrected his passion. His manhood throbbed to life again. But Konal bit his tongue and refused to spoil the sweet moment.

"I've never slept underneath the trees and starry sky," she said. "I've always known the security of my home or the safety of a friend's cottage. Tis not easy for me to be here, milord. But if I must endure all these new things, I am grateful for your protection."

He squeezed his eyes shut, almost helpless to resist kissing her. Her words were sweeter than honey, nearly as enticing as the curves of her body. "You mustn't say such things, Silvia."

She turned over then. "Why?"

He gazed at her pretty face, committing her features to memory. "Some men would misinterpret your words as seductive."

"But truth should never be withheld. Not when it burdens your heart. Not when you owe someone a debt of gratitude for saving your life."

"I didn't save you," he said.

"I would have slept through the fire," she offered. "Believe me, milord. And you've defended me against the Danes." She swallowed hard. "The image of that severed head will never leave me."

"Ulf deserved to die a long time ago."

"But you killed him for me. And though murder is a great sin, my god forgives you if you were truly protecting an innocent."

Protecting an innocent, yes, but his selfish motivation bordered on evil in her faith. He wanted Silvia for himself. And knowing dozens of men lusted after her was eating him up inside. Just thinking about it drove him mad.

"Roll over, Silvia. Go to sleep." It served more as a warning, for if he gazed upon her a second more, he'd take liberties and taste her plump lips again and again.

She did as he bid, and Konal knew if he survived this night, he could face anything thereafter. For the girl had bewitched him.

"Good night, Jarl Konal," she said.

Another wish had been fulfilled. She'd finally said his name.

Chapter Fourteen

THE WIND WHIPPED through Silvia's unbound hair as she stood at the edge of the cliffs overlooking the North Sea. How beautiful she looked, eyes full of wonder. Konal had never watched someone gazing upon the ocean for the first time. But he shared her fascination, for it had been seven months since he'd beheld the angry gray waves or seen the sails of a longship.

"Now I understand," she said softly, looking at him.

"Understand what?"

"Why your people aspire to master something so untamed and wholly beautiful. God's hands are mighty."

"Aye," he agreed. "There is nothing more mesmerizing, more unexplored, more perfect than the sea. On a good day, she'll open up to you like a woman in love, granting access to the most exotic places. But when she rages, her angry depths will swallow you. And she never gives up her dead, Silvia."

"Then I will admire her from a safe distance," she said.

He chuckled at her logic, knowing if she ever stepped upon a Norse vessel, she'd conquer her fear.

"Prince Ivarr mentioned your father's ship."

"Yes," he said. "But it isn't anchored here. I must travel further north."

"Oh." She sounded disappointed.

"Did you hope to see the boat that would carry me away

from your homeland?"

"I've seen sketches of longships, even watched the sails mended in Jorvik. But I've never glimpsed one in the water."

He disliked the feeling that came over him then, the desire to fulfill any of her wishes, and the need to make her smile. Remembering who she was should set his mind straight. A slave. A bloody Saxon. An enemy. But as he studied her, her birthright didn't matter. For she'd outshine most women in his homeland. Even the Danes noticed it. This girl's future was better than most. She'd not end up a bed slave. Silvia would attract a powerful man, a warrior worthy of her heart and admiration.

"We must go now," he said.

"So soon?" Her lips curved downward. "We've only just arrived."

"And lost a full day by taking the long way. If there's any hope of finding Jahn or the men who besieged our camp, I must get to my steading and take inventory. Count the able-bodied men in my service and possibly recruit fighters from the nearby steadings."

"So you will avenge the men who died?"

"I will trade blood for blood."

She walked away from the cliffs and moved to the horses tethered together. Petting their necks affectionately, she whispered in their ears.

"You like horses?" he asked.

"All animals," she answered.

"But me."

She smiled. "Another regret I have. Know I insulted you out of anger and fear. Anyone in my situation would have done the same, milord."

"I understand too well."

"You aren't a mindless beast."

"Just a heartless one?" His eyebrows shot up.

"Must I answer now?"

"You require more time to think about it?"

"Having learned a valuable lesson before, I would choose not to rush to judgment again."

Odin have mercy. He'd never met a woman like her. She'd openly insulted one of the most bloodthirsty princes of Scandinavia and lived. Her wit and beauty put him at a clear disadvantage. Konal knew distance was the only cure for the fever that was slowly setting in.

"You will ride alone today."

Hours later, they arrived at the border of his lands, demarcated by two white stones with his name carved upon their face.

"Jarl Konal the Red," she said out loud. "Even the breadth of your borders is described."

"You can decipher the runes?"

"I can read the most rudimentary symbols."

"And which direction shall we ride to reach my house?"

"Northeast," she said. "I see smoke in the distance."

"Aye," he agreed, yet again impressed by her abilities.

A sheep path cut through the lush fields, then slowly meandered up a hillside. It was from the top that he first spied his holdings clearly. A cluster of thatch-roofed cottages located near a stream waited below. Sheep and horses grazed in an open pasture. And people were working in what Konal presumed were his gardens.

"Prince Ivarr has rewarded you well," she observed. "The land is prosperous."

With renewed excitement, he kicked his steed down the incline, more than ready to claim his property. Two men waited in front of the main cottage as he rode closer.

"Greetings, milord," one of the strangers said. "I am Fiske, your caretaker."

"A Norseman?" Konal dismounted, shocked to meet a countryman. "How did you know who I was?"

"We received word of your arrival days ago," he said. "As for my presence, I was chosen by Prince Ivarr himself. A request for a volunteer from amongst our troops stationed far north of Jorvik came. I answered the call, after being promised my family could join me."

The news pleased Konal and he grasped the man's arm in friendship. "Your wife and children are here?"

"Settled a month ago."

"And you?" Konal eyed the other man, knowing he was Saxon.

"Alfred." He bowed.

"How long have you been here?"

"This is the only home I've ever known, milord. My father and grandfather were smithies."

Never quick to trust, he'd treat the man with respect until he had a chance to speak to Fiske about him.

"Have any travelers passed this way?" He returned his attention to the Norseman, hoping his attackers had ventured here in search of him.

"No, milord. We rarely receive visitors. But if you require a messenger or wish someone to go to the market for supplies, there are twenty men ready to serve. And we house ten families in the guest cottages."

"And the stable?" Konal wanted to examine the horses. Prince Ivarr was always in need of superior horse flesh. If the stock proved hale, it could be profitable to breed them.

"One of the sturdiest structures on the farm. Do you want to see it now or would you prefer to get settled first?" Fiske gazed at Silva, still perched on her horse.

Gesturing for his new friend to come closer, Konal shot a quick look at Silvia. "The lady is to be treated with honor. Though a thrall, I hold her in high regard. Assign one of the girls to serve as her maid. As for me, food and mead. I will meet my servants today, but not on an empty stomach."

"As you wish, milord."

Satisfied Fiske would follow his instructions, Konal returned to the horses and helped Silvia down.

"Did I overhear correctly?" she asked. "Your servant is from Norway?"

"Aye. The gods have once again favored me."

He escorted her to the entrance of the abundant cottage that would be his temporary home. Inside, the central room served as the kitchen and hall. Constructed of wattle and daub as most structures in Northumbria, the south facing wall was made of gray stone. A fire pit with an iron kettle hanging over it was attended by an older woman. On the other side of the space, a trestle table with a dozen chairs offered the only seating. Several trunks lined the east wall.

"Tis clean," Silvia said. "And I am sure the stairs lead to the master's chamber."

"Aye," he said, accustomed to meager accommodations since he left Norway. "There is another doorway over there, perhaps a third room." He pointed. "I will make some changes here." Eventually Konal would ask his youngest brother to relocate and oversee the steading.

A few minutes later, Fiske joined them inside, with two women in tow. "Milord," he bowed. "My own daughter, Saga, has asked to serve your lady."

The girl stepped forward and curtsied. "Sir."

"Thank you." Konal smiled. "Silvia will be a kind mistress."

"And this is Queenie," Fiske introduced the second woman.

"Her grandmother is the cook. But the old bird is deaf, so Queenie stays close by."

Both women wore homespun dresses, patched and a drab brown color. And judging by their spare figures, they could use more sustenance. The bloody Saxons starved their servants. "I don't want to interfere with your duties. Tis better to carry on as you would. Queenie..." he started. "Instruct your grandmother to serve a morningtide meal. Some bread and milk, and cheese if there's enough."

"Two meals for us?" she asked, surprised.

"Yes. I can't afford for my servants to blow away in the wind."

The girl grinned appreciatively and immediately went to her grandmother.

Next he addressed Saga. "Is that a second bedchamber over there?"

"Yes, sir. A small one."

"Have one of the stable boys help unpack the bags from the horses outside, then you and Silvia can get settled."

"I will sleep here, milord?" she asked.

"Aye. Are you prepared to leave your family?"

"I am ready to do anything you ask, sir."

"Good."

Fiske beamed with pride and patted his daughter's face affectionately. "She's an obedient child, milord. You need only direct her hands."

"I expect a meal set out within the hour," he told Silvia. "Until then, I will be in the stables."

Konal followed his servant outside, determined to make his new steading efficient and profitable. Ivarr had been generous to a fault, likely trying to entice him to stay on the island. For once he left, Konal planned on never returning. And now that he'd surmised his holdings, he hoped Silvia would agree to live here. She'd be safe and, in time, maybe happy.

If Fiske had a capable son, a marriage might be in Silvia's future.

Chapter Fifteen

On the fifth night at the farm, Konal instructed Silvia to prepare for a feast he was holding for his tenants. In order to foster loyalty and peace, he thought it worth the cost of a few fattened sheep and fresh vegetables. He expected her to wear one of the gowns Prince Ivarr had gifted her with and would sit with him at the high table. All in the name of establishing her as an important part of his new household. An honored position for any slave—as he so aptly reminded her before she went to her room to dress.

The idea of belonging to someone, the way livestock or property did, hadn't sunk in. Nor would it. Freedom remained her true goal, the inspiration needed to wake every day with purpose. For the sooner she won her master's trust and respect, the quicker she was sure he'd let her go. Then she could return to York with the scrolls, repair her cottage, and live the life of a recluse, or join a convent. The monks would give her letters of recommendation, maybe even find a cloister nearby so they could visit on holy days.

Saga encouraged her to sit on the stool so the girl could arrange her long hair. "If you wish to please the jarl, let me braid the sides of your hair in Norse fashion."

She gazed at the girl, tempted to say she wasn't a bloody Viking, but a Saxon. However, Saga had been so kind, staying close, and getting Silvia whatever she needed. "Do you think adorning my hair and body with pleasing things will help me win my freedom?"

She looked uncertain. "You wish to return to Jorvik?"

"I wish to return to my own life."

"Living amongst the Danes?"

"Nay," she said. "That is a tragedy I could do without. I miss the monks and my cottage. My garden and scrolls."

Saga pulled a comb through the tangles in her hair. "What use are written words? A woman need only concern herself with pleasing her family and finding a husband who will provide for her."

She couldn't fault the girl for her beliefs. She'd been raised as most women, to serve men without question. But Silvia's sire had given her a rare gift—knowledge—and nothing would keep her from it. Not even an axe-wielding giant.

"I'm afraid you will find me a great disappointment, Saga. My desires are not the same as yours. Of course I've dreamed of marriage and children, hoping to someday meet the kind of man who would appreciate my talents. But once they find out I possess the skills of a scribe, they disappear."

"Jarl Konal hasn't abandoned you."

She met the maid's gaze. "No. But there is a reason for that … I am a thrall."

"No man has ever watched me the way our master watches you."

Silvia chuckled. "He fears I'll run away, nothing more."

Saga's deft fingers worked quickly, leaving four tight braids on either side of Silvia's face, with tiny gold beads on the ends.

"And now for the dress," she said, walking to the narrow bed where a purple gown had been laid out. "The embroidery is the best I've ever seen." Saga held it up.

Silvia slipped out of her wool garment and allowed the maid to pull the new dress over her head. The soft linen felt good against her skin. Once the laces were tied, the maid stepped back and looked her over carefully.

"Once our master sees you in this, I think you might change your mind about why he watches you so closely. And if the jarl is only interested in keeping you here, then my brothers will surely compete for your attention."

"Brothers?"

"Aye," she said. "Both fishermen in Norway. But once we came here, they were forced to learn farming and how to tend sheep."

"Do you miss your country?"

"Aye."

"Then surely you can sympathize with me—Jorvik is the only place I've ever lived. No matter how kind Jarl Konal is to me, or how helpful you are, I long for the familiar sights and sounds of my own home. So many have died, and now more than ever…" Tears burned her eyes, but she wiped them away, realizing her words were lost on a girl from the very place her captor came from.

"Why did you stop speaking?" Saga asked.

"Some thoughts are better left unsaid, Saga. I am a Saxon. You are Norse. Your loyalties will always be to the jarl and your family."

"That doesn't mean we cannot be friends."

"Maybe," she said. "But it surely signifies our limits. You will be expected to report anything suspicious I say to Konal."

The maid nodded. "Yes."

Someone knocked on the door then. "Jarl Konal wants you to come out," a man called.

Silvia sighed. Unaccustomed to wearing such finery, she felt as if she were in an entertainer's costume instead of a gown. She walked to the door and opened it, finding a stranger waiting for her. He bowed.

"I will escort you to the table," he said.

The hall had been transformed. Torch stands were positioned in the corners, illuminating the space in soft light. Bundles of flowers tied together with colorful ribbons decorated the walls. A second trestle table had been set up on the far side of the room and that's where Konal waited. As she passed by the men and women at the lower table and standing about, they acknowledged her with smiles or a bend of the head.

What had the jarl done to prepare his servants to accept the daughter of a scribe from Jorvik as an honored guest? For though most of his tenants shared her blood, the leaders in York often overtaxed farmers, creating deep contention.

Konal stood once she reached the table. "Silvia." His eyes gleamed with desire.

She curtsied, then greeted the men and women at the high table. All members of Saga's family, including her two brothers.

Seated to Konal's left, she accepted a cup of mead from him. "Thank you," she said, taking a tentative sip.

He leaned close. "The color of your gown suits you, Silvia. But I'm afraid it makes me want to rip it off your perfect body."

This time she gulped the mead, needing something to steady her nerves. Whenever he spoke so boldly, her blood boiled. His hands and lips were temptations she knew she must resist.

Freshly bathed, beard trimmed, and wearing a dark tunic with breeches, the jarl appeared a new man. A thick silver chain hung about his neck, matching bracelets on his wrists.

"I could say the same to you, milord." Perhaps if she returned his sentiments with equal ardor, he'd cease teasing her.

His eyebrows rose and he studied her closely. "Is that an

offer?"

"Tis merely a compliment. I have never seen you without armor."

"Then I thank you," he said. "But remember, I have seen you without clothes and prefer it over any of the finery Ivarr has given you."

Her cheeks flushed, but gratefully, the women serving the meal approached the table, stopping the conversation.

"Milord," Queenie spoke. "The meat is ready."

Six trenchers were placed on the two tables, filled with mutton and gravy. Fresh bread, beans, carrots, and turnips were also offered. The jarl helped himself first, filling his plate, then cut a generous piece of meat for Silvia. A servant refilled his cup with mead and he sampled it, then stood up, raising his vessel high.

"Tonight, I open my home to all of you not only as your master, but as a friend. Those who live in peace thrive. War has crippled this land. Violence has claimed thousands of lives, Northmen and Saxons alike. But here, away from Jorvik and the bloody Danes, I offer you another way to live. I will not condemn you if you don't judge me. I will protect you from the swords of your enemies if you swear allegiance to the house of Konal the Red. These lands will always hold a special place in my heart for it marks the beginning of a new time for me. I am no longer just a second son, but a jarl. And I protect what I care for."

She didn't miss the quick look her master gave her at the same time he said those last words. The same promise he'd made her before, only now it extended to the families living on his steading. And once again, Silvia found herself caught up in the passion he exuded, believing every word her natural born enemy spoke.

"After you have filled your stomachs and drank your mead

and wine, I will offer all the men in this room the chance to take an oath of allegiance. Those who refuse are free to go."

Applause followed and Konal grinned. "Aye," he continued. "Let the whole bloody world burn down around us, but peace will be kept under this roof." He sat down again, scooping her hand off the table and gave it a squeeze. "Did I not promise to take care of you?"

She nodded.

"And do you accept the challenge of being mistress of this house?"

"I will do whatever you ask, milord."

"Including considering a match between you and one of those men sitting over there?" He gestured at Saga's brothers.

The question shocked her. A match? What did he mean exactly? "A marriage?"

"Aye."

"How much mead have you drank, milord?"

Konal's rich laughter filled the room. "Not enough to cloud my mind, Silvia. Surely you know I will leave this place soon. Once I am satisfied with the improvements and trust the men managing my affairs, I will resume my life in Norway. Knowing you are safe has become an important part of my plans."

"B-but…"

"Wait." He held his hand up, stopping her. "Do not ask me to send you back to Jorvik. The moment we met, your fate changed forever. And though I may not have the privilege of being an active part of your life, the gods have revealed to me what I must do to safeguard your future. If you marry a Norseman, no one outside of these walls will ever know you're a Saxon. For in this household, you will always be regarded as part of my family."

She didn't know what to say. One minute he was pawing at

her, kissing her, fondling her body with hunger, the next, offering her protection and a husband? Should she take his concern as a compliment or utter rejection?

"Milord..." The words wouldn't come.

"Have I surprised you?" he asked.

"Days ago you wanted to kill me."

"Days ago you gave me every reason to seek your end."

"What has changed?" she asked, finding the courage to look him in the eyes.

"Me."

Dear God in heaven. No man had ever shared his intimate feelings with her. And judging by the tone of his voice and the expression on his face, he meant it. She'd influenced him in some way and he cared for her.

"Our short history together is tainted with hatred and violence."

"I forgive you," he said.

A chill spiraled up her spine as she continued to stare into the depths of his dark blue eyes. If a heathen understood the meaning of forgiveness, what else did he know?

Chapter Sixteen

AFTER THE MEAL ended, the tables were moved aside, and two men with flutes performed. At first, everyone congregated in the center of the hall, listening in silence. Konal wanted to show these people how to enjoy their time together. Music shouldn't be wasted. Eyeing Silvia beside him, he slipped his arm about her waist. She smiled up at him, her sweet lips ready for hot kisses. But he'd spare her in public and, instead, guided her to an open space between the musicians and crowd.

He bowed before her, then took her hands in his, showing her how to step to the melody.

"You dance?" she asked.

"I do many things."

He twirled her around, then reclaimed her tiny body, his palms momentarily rested on her hips. It didn't take long for Fiske to lead his wife in the same Norse dance, then soon several couples followed. The men and women who chose not to participate, clapped their hands enthusiastically.

After several songs, the color in Silvia's cheeks only made her more beautiful. Breathless, she stepped back from Konal.

"I am in need of a drink."

"I will not permit you to stop yet." He turned and waved at someone across the room.

Seconds later, one of Saga's brothers joined them. Konal

introduced him. "Silvia, this is Gunnar, the eldest of Fiske's children."

The broad-shouldered man bowed. "I am honored to meet you."

She eyed both men nervously. "I am winded, milord. Must I…"

"Saga will bring you some water."

A new chorus began and Gunnar swept her away from Konal.

As he watched them lean and sway, the sight of her in another man's arms pierced his heart. His personal feelings didn't matter though. Keeping her safe did. Looking away, he strutted back to the high table and asked Saga to take Silvia a drink.

"She is a delicate girl. But my son likes the idea of marriage suddenly." Fiske stood beside him.

"What man wouldn't for a bride as ripe as Silvia?"

His countryman rubbed his chin. "And has she been plucked?"

Although a legitimate question, it angered Konal. "The answer is for the girl to give to the man that wins her hand."

"Aye, milord."

"Am I to understand that one of your sons is ready to accept my terms? Whoever the girl chooses will receive thirty acres of land and enough money to build a cottage suitable for Silvia to live in and to furnish it."

"A more generous offer than we expected."

"And you'll welcome her as a daughter, protecting her at all costs?"

"I swear upon Odin's eye."

Konal gripped the man's shoulder. "After this melody ends, send your other son to dance with her." He turned to go.

"Wait, Jarl Konal."

"What is it?"

"If I may speak freely…"

"Permission granted."

"After raising six children of my own, it is my duty to sense when something upsets them. You are only a few years older than my firstborn. If you love the girl, why don't you marry her?"

Konal growled, displeased his servant had spoken *too* freely. "I've never claimed to feel anything."

Fiske smirked. "A blind fool could see the attraction you share."

"Physical need doesn't mean I love her. Any man would be tempted by her beauty and fiery spirit. But for your sake, Fiske, I will answer plainly. Even if I wished to keep her, my family wouldn't accept her. As a slave or concubine maybe, and I refuse to expose her to the cruel world any foreigner faces in our homeland. The Trondelag is full of vicious people who look for any reason to spill the blood of a Saxon. You should know this as well as I."

"But you are the son of a jarl."

"And obligated to my father until I establish my own house."

"I understand, milord."

With a last longing look at Silvia, Konal grabbed a wineskin off the wall near the door and went outside. A dip in the creek's cold water would help calm his jealousy.

SEATED BETWEEN BOTH of Fiske's attentive sons, Silvia tried to be friendly. Gunnar had green eyes and blond hair, his brother Tarben had darker coloring like his mother. But neither could keep her attention like Konal. Occasionally, she mentally blocked out their voices and scanned the room for the jarl.

She'd watched him leave over an hour ago and his continued absence worried her.

Tarben offered her another cup of mead.

"No," she said. "I've had three already—enough to make it hard to walk a straight path."

He grinned. "You can lean upon my arm so you won't stumble."

"And mine," Gunnar added.

"If you'd be so kind as to excuse me." She stood up, intent on searching for Konal. "I would like to take a short walk, alone."

The tenants gathered outside wished her well as she headed for the back of the cottage. A footpath led to the creek, the place she guessed Konal would be. She found him lounging on the ground, staring at the evening sky. Not wanting to disturb him, she stopped a few feet behind him and waited for him to acknowledge her presence.

"You've found me," he finally said.

The man surely had eyes in the back of his head. "Aye."

"Did Fiske's handsome sons disappoint you?"

"Both are determined to win my affection."

He repositioned himself so he could see her, lying on his side. "Do you favor one yet?"

She thought about it. If she said no, he'd force them upon her again and again until she chose one. If she lied, it might earn her more time to convince him to set her free. "Yes."

He sat up then, his eyes narrowed on her. "Which?"

"Gunnar."

"Wisely chosen. First born sons receive the greatest shares of their father's wealth."

"Is that what you think interests me?"

"If it didn't, I'd consider you a foolish girl."

His casual manner hurt her in ways she couldn't describe. "Please don't make me marry someone I don't love."

"Love?" He crossed his arms over his chest. "A childish notion."

"No, it isn't."

"You have a vivid imagination, Silvia. Your future husband will surely appreciate the years of entertainment you will provide. But in the real world, where men and women die every day from starvation or war, love is the last thing they look for in a marriage. You require the protection a Norse name can give you. A secure home. Children to deepen your bond with Fiske's family. If love is in your future, it will come in time."

"When did you lose faith in love, milord? After Eira died?"

Even in the fading light she could see the change in his features. Rage flashed in his eyes. He stood up, taking a defensive posture. "What right have you to speak her name? Didn't I forbid it?"

She trembled then, a kernel of fear burst inside her stomach. "If you expect me to bend to your will, sir, then I deserve the truth. How can you force me into a marriage I do not want if you can't explain why you don't believe in a love match?"

He sucked in a ragged breath. "I've already explained the purpose of marriage."

"I don't wish to share a bed with a man who doesn't love me."

"Passion will warm your bed."

She shook her head, refusing to accept it. "I want more."

"You can't have it," he said sternly.

She whirled around, hiding the tears that wet the corners of her eyes. "Tell me about Eira."

"Curse you, woman." He grabbed her arms. "She is alive and well."

"If the woman you love is alive, why did you kiss me, milord? Why did you try to seduce me?"

Konal turned her around, his forehead nearly touching hers. "A man can love one woman and want to fuck another."

His words sickened her. "You were right about one thing, milord," she said in a controlled tone, her stomach in knots. "I am a fool, *for believing in you.*" She pushed him away with all her strength and ran in the direction of the hills, desperate to find a place where she could be alone.

Chapter Seventeen

KONAL DIDN'T MOVE a muscle—he'd never meant to hurt her, only to put her off emotionally, *and* protect himself more than anything. But the pained expression on her pretty face told him he'd had a serious lapse in judgment. He eyed the empty wineskin. Blaming potent drink would be a sad excuse for bad behavior. But what did Silvia expect? For him to drop down on a knee and confess undying love and devotion? It just wasn't possible.

All his instincts told him to walk away, go inside, and send one of Fiske's sons to fetch her back to the gathering. Let them deal with her now. Her welfare rested on their shoulders.

Or did it?

It was then he knew his own future wasn't as clear as it had been a week ago.

Something about Silvia had penetrated the armor-clad layers of his heart. Even thousands of miles of ocean couldn't change that. With a frustrated sigh, he strode across the field, headed in the direction of where she'd gone. She must be made to see the value in marrying someone who could protect her. And while he expected some resistance, Konal knew how to bring the stubborn girl to heel.

Simple words weren't enough, nor the threat of another spanking. She must see it in his eyes and hear the resoluteness of his voice at the same time.

He found her sitting underneath a tree, back resting against the thick trunk with her head bowed.

"Why did you follow me?" she asked without looking up.

"Come back, it's growing dark. I can't allow you to stay outside by yourself. The men who attacked us may be waiting for the right moment to strike again."

"That's what worries you?" She met his gaze then, palming tears off her face.

"Aye."

"Then leave me alone, milord."

"Don't misjudge my words, Silvia. I care enough to see you settled before I go."

She momentarily closed her eyes like she was trying to gather her wits. "I thought you were an honorable man."

"I am."

She laughed bitterly. "Men under your command killed my father—though I'll never know who. You refuse to send me home. Yet you also saved my life twice, milord. I'm very confused. Resentful that you wish to imprison me here."

Losing patience, he growled. "Get up, Silvia."

"I prefer to stay under the shelter of this tree. Surely there's a willing bedmate amongst your servants who would gladly *fuck* you."

Coming from her mouth, those words ripped through him more fatally than a blade. "You're bitter because I loved another woman."

Her eyes lit up. "Hardly." She stared at his crotch, then shook her head. "You overestimate the value of what's between your legs."

Did the wench remember everything he said? He'd told her something very similar in Jorvik. Only he didn't mean it then or now. "Why do you still defy me, Silvia? Your life is in my hands. I can do whatever I wish with you. Kiss you. Caress you. Embrace you…"

"Rape me."

"Kill you," he emphasized.

She gasped at his harsh words but rose, determined to show him how she felt. Standing directly in front of him, she swept her hair over her right shoulder and offered her slim, white neck. "I see you carry many blades at your hip. Please … choose one and put me out of my misery finally. Let all this end. Send me to meet my god and sire. For surely it would be a better end for me than being forced to stay here and live a lie."

Spoken like a true Valkyrie—he could see her wearing the golden armor, a shield and sword in her hands, standing before Odin himself, arguing endlessly. She didn't fear death. He held her steely gaze, pressure building inside his chest.

"Well, milord?"

"How could you ask me to do that?" Instead, he tugged her close and slanted his mouth across hers, catching her tongue between his lips, taking what he'd wanted more than anything. Another taste of Silvia. Possibly his last, for after tonight, she might belong to another man.

He kissed her passionately, his fingers wandering freely, seeking the softest places on her body. He loved her intensity, the way she fought for what she believed in. And her scent … it never failed to put him in a daze. Surprisingly, his little Valkyrie in the flesh didn't resist. She clung to him, her tiny hands slipping up his arms, then laced together behind his neck. She leaned into him, her full breasts pressed against his chest.

"This must be an abomination," she whispered at last. "For how can I offer myself so freely to a man who thinks me no better than a slave?"

She couldn't be more wrong. He tried to recover from the intimacy, his mind muddled by more than excessive mead drinking. "I hold you in higher regard than I do most women."

"Then prove it," she challenged. "Set me free."

"Never." He must always know where she was. If he let her go, she'd disappear forever, and likely die at the hands of a bloody Dane. "You belong to me."

"I belong to no man," she spit.

"Wrong again." He gripped her arm and gave her a gentle shake. "I assure you, I'm as real as any man can be, Silvia. Surely you can attest to that—your hungry fingers once caressed my bollocks with enthusiasm."

"Pig."

He grinned proudly. "So I am."

She jerked free and turned around, then took two steps before Konal, consumed by anger and protectiveness, swept her into his arms.

"Did I not tell you before? Your mind is no longer your own. Don't move unless I give you permission. Don't think without my approval."

She kicked and struggled to get away, but Konal held on, his breeches getting tighter from arousal. There was no relief. Not in Northumbria. All he could envision was stripping her, laying her across his bed, and showing her how he really felt. All that pent up aggression and frustration would bleed out of him the moment he filled her with his seed.

But he'd already offered her hand to one of Fiske's sons. Taking her maidenhead would only complicate things.

So instead of doing what his mind and body screamed for, he carried her inside the hall. The music stopped and all his guests watched as he kicked her chamber door open and dropped her on the bed.

"You will spend the rest of the night in here. Think about the way you speak to me before you dare come out in the morning. All my patience and good cheer is spent, Silvia. In the morn, you will present yourself in the hall, ready to choose a husband."

He didn't bother giving her a chance to respond. He slammed her door shut and directed one of his men to stand guard through the night.

"Bring me more mead," he demanded as he strutted to the high table. "And more music. I would watch the girls dance. And enjoy the banter of the men."

CHRIST IN HEAVEN. The constant struggle with Konal had finally caught up with Silvia. Exhausted, she turned on her side and tucked her knees into her chest. Even breathing normally felt like a challenge. How could she ever face these people again?

Konal had humiliated her beyond belief.

Instead of letting her sorrow come out in the form of tears, she rolled off the bed and walked to the corner of her room where her leather bag sat. As if summoned by the angels, she opened it and rummaged around until she found the treasure her father had left her. The scrolls.

By the light of the single wall torch, she broke the seal on the first missive, praying she'd chosen the right time to do so.

After reading the first few lines, she looked away, took a deep breath, then stared at the page again, emotions swelling inside her chest. This wasn't a sacred text, but a personal letter from her sire. It spoke of her earliest years in the monastery. How much joy she brought him. It attested to his undying love as a father. How all the monks celebrated her young life and curiosity.

"How much we all love you," she read aloud. "From the moment you were permitted entry into the scriptorium, you wandered endlessly, touching everything reverently, as if you knew how priceless the missives were..."

She set the precious letter aside, then opened another one, finding the same—inspirational writings from her sire. All about their lives together. The next one described her mother, told of the happiness they shared while she carried her in the womb. "Our very own piece of heaven on earth," her father had written. "When I rest my hand on your mother's swollen belly and feel you move within, I am reminded of the gift of life. How delicate it is, but how boldly we must live it. Never afraid to do what is right in the eyes of God. And never ashamed of our faith in Christ..."

The tears blinded her and she dropped to her knees, overwhelmed by emotions. Love and hatred collided in her chest.

The door to her room opened, but Silvia didn't care who stood behind her. Painful waves of sorrow wracked her body.

"What is it, Silvia?" Saga's sweet voice sounded.

She held up the scroll, knowing the poor girl couldn't read. "Everything I ever wondered about, all the doubts and hopes I've ever had, have been answered amongst these pages. And there's nothing I can do to bring my father back and tell him how much I love him."

Inconsolable, she crawled back to her bed, hoping she'd fall asleep and never awaken again.

Chapter Eighteen

A LOUD NOISE pulled Silvia from her sleep. But as she shot up from her bed, the ear-piercing scream she heard made her freeze. Saga slept on a pallet on the floor and the girl was missing. Another shout came, this time from a man inside the hall, which made her think twice about opening her door. So did Konal's earlier instructions to not come out until the morning. From the small, square window on the far wall, she could see the darkness. Still nighttime.

But what if someone had gotten hurt?

Cautious, she lifted the latch and peeked through. Men were scrambling for the entrance, some with weapons. As she started to exit her chamber, Saga appeared and gently pushed her back inside.

"No," she cautioned as she shut the door behind her. "Please, stay here. Jarl Konal forbid me to let you leave this room. We must wait for his command."

Head still swimming from the fight she had earlier with Konal, she tried to grasp what her maid was saying. "What is going on, Saga? Are we under attack?"

Saga's expression seemed guarded and she folded her hands, looking unsure of what to say and do. "Several sheep were slaughtered in the closest field. And there's a fire. Two of the guest cottages have been burned down."

Silvia blinked at her, remembering the fire in the middle of the night when she was traveling with Konal. He'd saved her life and now she must do the same for him. "Stay if you wish," she said with deep conviction. "But I will not hide while these people face their deaths. My hands are as capable as any."

She took a step toward the door, but Saga shifted to the right, blocking her path.

"What are you doing?" Silvia asked, shocked by her interference.

"What our master bid me do. I'm responsible for your life."

She exhaled a harsh breath. Everything had gone quiet in the hall and panic started to set in. "Do you hear anything beyond that door?" Silvia asked.

"Nothing."

"Tis a bad sign. What if your father or brothers are hurt? Will you be able to live with yourself if you lose one of them?" She hoped her words convinced Saga to move, because the next option was physical confrontation. And though her maid was quite a bit taller and likely stronger, Silvia's motivations were greater, for she'd felt the sting of loss recently, and that made her desperate.

A fresh wave of grief washed over her as she waited for Saga to make up her mind.

"Please…"

"Odin will punish me if anything happens to you." She stepped aside.

Without a word, Silvia rushed from her room, ran through the hall, and outside. Women and children were gathered near the southeast corner of the cottage and she didn't hesitate to question them.

"Where is Jarl Konal?"

A woman pointed toward the fields. "Beyond the gardens

with the other men."

"Thank you."

"Wait," the woman said. "We were told to…"

Silvia didn't care.

Minutes later, breathless and hidden amongst the trees, she watched in abject terror as Konal and several of his men battled a group of attackers. There were at least seven. She covered her mouth, too tempted to call out to the man she realized she loved. Why had it taken so long to admit it? Only when faced with losing him did her heart open up.

She then bowed her head, humbling herself before God. "Spare him. Please. The world is a better place with him in it…"

"A touching sentiment," a male voice said as he grabbed her arm. "So another beauty surrenders her heart to my arrogant cousin."

Forced to turn around, Silvia found a familiar face—Hallam.

"You're responsible for this violence?" she asked.

"Yes. I've waited a lifetime to regain my honor from Konal. And now that I have you, he'll have no choice but to surrender."

With a cry, she clawed his face.

"Bitch…" he screamed, squeezing her wrist and holding on tight. "Once my cousin is dead, I'll teach you a life changing lesson." Then he slapped her face so hard she saw stars before her eyes.

Startled, she touched her cheek with her free hand but didn't make a sound. She'd never give this man the satisfaction of hearing her pain. *Betraying bastard…*

As Hallam dragged her into the open, she searched for Konal. The sound of weapons crashing together and the grunts and moans sent a chill up her spine. Two men were lying on the ground already, unmoving. Once again violence and death surrounded her. Where was Konal?

"I won't let you hurt him," she said. She landed a solid blow to his cheek, then tried to hit him again.

But he was faster and stronger, and pulled her against his chest. Then he spun her around and locked her in place by wrapping his arm about her neck. "Move and I'll choke the life out of you." He demonstrated by applying pressure to her throat. "It wouldn't take much to kill you, girl."

How she hated feeling helpless and useless. If she'd only listened to Saga and stayed in her room… Now Hallam would use her as leverage against Konal.

They walked slowly to the center of the field, the bright moonlight as revealing as a bonfire.

"Hear me, Konal the Red," Hallam pronounced.

As if he'd cast a spell, the fighting quickly stopped.

Her gaze moved swiftly across the line of men standing nearby and she found her Viking with an axe in each hand, a maddened expression on his face. His eyes went wide when he spied her, then surmised his cousin.

"All these years I've waited for the moment to bring you to your knees, Konal."

"You couldn't pay a whore to kneel before you, what makes you think I will?" He squared his shoulders and took a step forward. "Coward. You'd use a woman as a shield? Let her go and face me as any warrior would. I'll even give you first strike."

Laughter sounded from the men, but Silvia didn't pay attention to anyone else but her master. As he came closer, she could see his sweat-slicked hair and blood-streaked face—poised to claim his next victim.

"Stand down," Hallam said, bringing a dagger to her throat. "Another step and I'll cut her. I already sacrificed Jahn and your other guard to the gods to win their favor. Imagine what I will get if I give them something as pure as this girl."

Konal raised his hands. "Tell me what to do."

"Drop your weapons."

His axes hit the ground with a thud.

"Now tell your men to do the same."

"No," Konal refused. "I'll give up only if you let my men walk away."

"You're in no position to bargain with me."

"I'll fight you with my bare hands before I let you kill one of my tenants."

Neither man was willing to give in and Silvia shifted nervously on her feet—willing to die if it meant Konal lived. Hallam must have mistaken her movement as another attempt to escape, for he yanked her head back.

"Do you know how many times I told this little bitch to be still?" He gazed down at her. "Only minutes in my arms and I, too, am bewitched. Now I understand your obsession, cousin. She is unlike any other woman I've known." He licked her face, laughing as she jerked her head away in revulsion. "I'll agree to your terms on one condition." He eyeballed Konal. "Relinquish your rights to this thrall, in front of all of these witnesses."

Konal growled like a rabid dog, and in a flash, a knife pierced Hallam's forehead. A strangled sound came out of his mouth and he stumbled backward, his hold on Silvia loosened. She wriggled free and dropped to her knees, watching in horror as Hallam collapsed.

She couldn't see anything after that, only heard someone yell it was over.

As the tears fell, she covered her face with both hands, ready to die for her disobedience. Everything Konal had done was for her. From claiming her in Jorvik, to bringing her here. The empty threats had been his way of protecting her, to convince her to do as he said so she'd live, not so he could kill her spirit.

"Silvia."

"Please..." she whispered. "Don't make me look at you. I am not worthy of your protection any longer."

"I'll be the judge of that," Konal said, reaching down and lifting her by the shoulders. "Face me, Silvia."

She didn't have the strength to hold herself up any longer, but she obeyed, struggling to stay upright.

"Look me in the eyes, girl."

Ashamed, she raised her head.

"Why did you leave the shelter? Did you not see the other women and children? Tell me the truth."

What excuse could she give to make him understand that the idea of him disappearing out of her life would be the final event that would make her no longer want to live? She'd already given up so many times after her father died. But this felt so different, like she couldn't breathe. "I couldn't bear to think of you in such danger. I had to see for myself."

They stood in silence for what seemed forever before he spoke again. "What has changed, Silvia?"

"Me," she said.

Konal caught her just as her weary legs gave out.

Chapter Nineteen

THERE WAS NOTHING more to be done tonight. Though Konal had stayed at Silvia's bedside hoping she'd come to, she still slept. Thankfully, her pulse and breathing were steady. The shock must have stolen her strength, for the girl had collapsed in his arms once she admitted why she'd, once again, disobeyed him. But how could he fault her? She'd lost more than most. Her parents and freedom, and now she knew he'd slip from her life, too, left as nothing but a memory.

He stood and yawned, needing to seek his bed, too. In the morning, once his sweet thrall had recovered, he'd set things right, announce her engagement to Fiske's eldest son. With his conscience clear, he'd then ride to his father's waiting ship and sail to Norway, ready to embrace his new life as a jarl.

As he opened the door, Saga met him. "Is she well?"

"Asleep still," he said. "Stay with her. She'll need someone to comfort her when she awakens."

If only he could understand Silvia's intentions, why she refused to yield. Even with the danger to their lives eliminated tonight, Hallam and his band of rebels all dead, he imagined her challenging his every word. It made him smile as he stepped into his chamber. They'd lived the equivalent of a year in the span of two weeks. And still the moment he appreciated the most was when he faced her in the scriptorium.

How she hated him. That's when he decided to save her from the Danes. Though violence bloomed inside him like any Northman, he recognized her strength. Silvia deserved to live. Though he'd been tempted to choke the life out of her on more than one occasion.

He sighed as he slipped underneath the fur on his mattress. Her fate rested in the hands of his gods now—Odin, Thor, and maybe even Freyja would smile upon her. For that elusive deity rewarded the bravest of souls. And Silvia's pure heart and undeterred commitment to whatever she believed right made her one of the fiercest warriors he'd ever met.

"Grant me safe passage to the Trondelag, great Odin," he whispered as his eyes grew heavy. "Let my sire welcome me home. Let my sister and brothers take me in their arms and kiss my cheeks, honoring my return..."

Hours later, something made Konal roll out of bed and grab his sword off the floor. Tonight had been the first time since his arrival in Northumbria that he felt comfortable enough to sleep naked. Apparently he was mistaken, for he suspected that one of Hallam's men had escaped and waited until the household was asleep to attack again.

Crouched and ready to strike, he waited for the right moment.

"Milord?" Silvia called gently. "Are you here?"

Konal closed his eyes, relieved and shocked that she'd come into his chamber in the middle of the night. "I am here." He relinquished his weapon, stashing it under the bed. "Are you ill?" He stood, finding her waiting in the middle of his spacious room.

"The fire has nearly gone out," she observed, gazing at the fire pit. "Shall I get some more wood from the hall?"

She must have noticed he wore no clothes. "Did you wander

into my room to check the fire, or is there something else bothering you, Silvia?"

"My mind and heart are greatly burdened," she admitted. "I couldn't go back to sleep and Saga is resting peacefully. I'd hoped to find you awake."

He rubbed his chin, purposely keeping his distance. She didn't need to see further proof of his hopeless attraction. Unfortunately, his manhood responded as it always did, standing at attention.

"Some bread and a cup of mead will settle your nerves," he said. "I will meet you in the hall."

"Thank you, milord," she said appreciatively. "But if I wanted to eat or recline in the hall, I wouldn't have risked coming to your room." She turned, focusing on his face.

"Do you have a confession to make? Some secret to share, my little Valkyrie?"

She nodded, her eyes never leaving his. "I want you to understand, sir. My father indulged me growing up. The monks rarely refused my wishes. So I never met a man like you. One who expected me to do as I was told without questioning him."

Though Konal didn't grasp the purpose of her words, he'd let her speak. "No man is without flaws."

"I have a bad habit of asking too many questions. And if I don't like the answers, well, I don't pay attention."

"You're still very young, Silvia. In time, perhaps you'll learn to respect the experience of your elders."

"I'm spoiled beyond measure."

"Girls often are."

"I wrongly accused you of murdering my father. Instead of seeking the truth, I let hatred blind me."

"Given the circumstances, I cannot hold you responsible for your actions."

"Milord?"

Konal wanted to hold her in his arms forever. "Aye?"

"Why did you keep me with you?"

There didn't seem to be a logical reason. "Because what man could resist you, Silvia? Tis not only your lovely form that intrigues me. There's heat in your eyes, hungry flames that threaten to devour the heart of any man who dares to love you."

"But not you. Konal the Red loves a woman he cannot have."

He waited for her to utter the forbidden name of the woman who betrayed him all those years ago. His betrothed. The witch who'd shattered his heart when he discovered her abed with a childhood friend.

"I love no one," he muttered.

"I love you," she said unshakably. "Tis why I ventured into your chamber. I overheard the guards outside speaking of your departure in the morn. You plan on visiting your father's men."

"Aye," he said, still unable to forget what she'd said. "My work is done here. Once I find out what we need for supplies, I'll return for a day, then sail home."

"And abandon me,"

"I leave you in capable hands," he pointed out. "With the kind of man I hope my own sister would choose as a husband."

"How fortunate for her." She stripped her dress off, then made quick work of her leggings.

By everything sacred… Had the girl lost her virginal mind? If she stayed here in her current state of undress for another second, Konal was sure he wouldn't be able to control himself. "Put your clothes back on, Silvia." He fought the animalistic urges threatening to break free inside him. "Why would you act so recklessly? There is no one who can protect you here. Above all, I am a man. A bloody Viking. A heathen who desires you more than any woman I've..."

She rushed into his arms, then reached up and cupped his cheeks, pulling his face to hers.

Konal sucked in a ragged breath, his heart consumed by the beautiful vision before him. Her dark hair cascaded over her shoulders, leaving her milky breasts completely exposed. So perfect in shape and size he wanted to caress and suckle them until his tongue withered. But he kept his hands fisted at his sides, still refusing to touch her. If the girl wanted to kiss him, she alone would be responsible.

When her velvety, hot tongue sought refuge in his mouth, he opened up to her on a deep moan. Another test from the gods? For he could think of no other reason why this sweet girl would tempt him.

"Konal?" she said. "Kiss me. Please."

"You don't know what you are asking." He captured her hands and locked them against his chest. "My need is driven by something dark and selfish. Wait until you take vows with Gunnar. Let him be the only man to ever make love to you."

She shook her head. "Reveal the truth. Do you tell your other thralls who to bed?"

He fell silent for a moment. Here was an example of the kind of questions she had been talking about earlier. Why did she persist? Why didn't she return to her room where she'd be safe? In the morning before he left, he'd announce her betrothal.

"Enough," he said too forcefully. "This cannot happen." He stepped back, preferring a dozen hard blows to the face over her possible reaction to his rejection.

Instead of giving up, Silvia reached out and caressed his shaft, then looked up at him expectantly. "Tis *my* choice."

All resistance faded. Konal lifted her hands to encircle his neck, tugging her close. "You understand what this means?

Tonight you belong to me, Silvia. And I'll kill the man who tries to take you away."

He swept her off her feet and carried her to the bed, fanning her out on the mattress. Before he lowered himself on top of her, he wanted to drink her in. He'd wrestled internally day and night to come up with reasons to stay away. And now, by her own offering, everything had changed. Damn reason and consequences.

His gaze drifted down her legs, so flawless and long, even her toes were pleasing.

"Konal," she breathed his name.

"Be patient," he urged. "I've waited a long time to see you this way. Too long."

He allowed himself the pleasure of tracing her shape with his fingertips—first her hip bone, then up her flat belly, ending with one of her pink nipples, which were already erect and ready for his mouth.

"Please…" she said, sounding so impatient.

He couldn't hold in the chuckle, loving her eagerness. "Let me help you." His hand moved between her legs, where he found wetness.

As his fingers slid inside her, she arched into him, moaning in pleasure. The surprise came when he used his thumb to deepen her enjoyment, circling her clitoris. Her eyes widened with wonder as he intensified the rhythm then slowed down, both discovering together what felt best to her.

"Do you like to be touched, little Valkyrie?" He'd do anything to provoke her into screaming his name. "Shall I do this?" He leaned across her chest and sucked one of her nipples into his mouth, biting it gently.

"What is happening to me?" she breathed out. "Will it hurt?"

"Not this part," he said. "My gift to you, sweet Silvia. For finding the courage to take what you want." He moved quickly, positioning himself between her legs and giving her a last look of deep admiration before he buried his face in her womanhood.

Her wet warmth covered his face and he tongued her gently at first, spreading her wider with his fingers. He ached with endless need for her. But not before he gave her a taste of what to expect. If she climaxed, she'd relax more, open up to him like a flower.

"Are you ready?" he asked, feeling the tension in her body.

"Aye."

With a last frenzied lick, she peaked in his mouth, shuddering against him. He slowly withdrew his fingers, desperate to possess her now. Joining her on the bed, he stretched out beside her, playing with a strand of her jet-colored hair—waiting to see what she'd do next.

She rolled onto her side, meeting his gaze. "I am speechless."

"Something I thought I'd never hear you say."

She slapped his arm playfully. "You twist the meaning of my words."

"Nay," he said. "I twisted my tongue inside your tight little mound."

When she caressed his cheek and scooted closer for a kiss, he pulled her on top of him. How perfect she felt fitted against him.

"Konal…" She studied his face. "I love you."

Though he'd never admit it, it felt good to hear those words again from someone he knew would never betray him. This innocent girl owned a heart worthy of his trust and love. But they were born enemies, cursed to remain master and thrall.

With the exception of tonight.

Instead of speaking, he fisted his hands in her long hair and forcefully pulled her into a lusty kiss. Just the brush of her soft skin against his chin made the hunger explode inside of him. He devoured her, their tongues swirled together in a wicked dance.

Silvia slid her hand downward and found his engorged shaft. She massaged the wet tip tenderly, nipping at his lips at the same time. The little vixen never failed to surprise him, in deed and word, and now in the bedchamber. With a guttural growl, he flipped her over, pinning her beneath him.

She writhed and moaned, her slick warmth rubbing against his cock. The time had arrived, no more waiting, no more excuses.

Using his knee to spread her legs wide, he positioned his shaft at her opening, then raised her arms above her head. "I've wanted you since the day I met you, Silvia. I will never forget the precious gift you offer me now." As he plundered her mouth, he thrust into her, pausing when he met some resistance inside her.

"Am I…"

"Shh." He released her arms and smoothed hair away from her face. "Tis natural," he assured her. "I am long and thick—more than your tiny body ever anticipated," he boasted. "As I've promised all along."

A smirk reached her sweet lips. "You didn't lie about your…"

He filled her completely, her muscles squeezing his length so tight he feared if he moved too fast he'd come. Nothing had ever felt better. And his heart ached now more than his bollocks. For in the morn… There was no use in regretting what they were doing. He loved her as much as she did him. Only he didn't have the courage to tell her. For if he confessed his deepest feelings, he'd never get on that boat and go home.

The only thing that had kept him alive so long in Northumbria, fighting as savagely as any Berserker, was the hope of reaching the shores of the Trondelag again. The land called to him like a songstress.

He shook the thoughts from his mind and gave Silvia what she demanded with an impatient wiggle of her hips. He hammered inside her hard and deep over and over again, consumed by her love.

"Do you feel it?" he whispered in her ear. "Do you feel what you do to me?"

With a roar, his hot seed filled her. But Konal was far from done. He slanted his mouth over hers and pumped his hips. "Come for me, little Valkyrie. And after you do, I'll show you how I can make love to you from behind."

Chapter Twenty

"WHAT DO YOU mean he's gone?" Silvia tried to remain calm. She never expected to hear this news when she returned to her room in the morning to change into a fresh dress.

As she always did, Saga was waiting for her.

"I am sorry," she said, casting her eyes downward. "He ate a simple meal, then returned to his chamber for nearly an hour. When he emerged, he was carrying his bags."

How had she slept through it? "Did he give you an explanation of any kind? Leave word for me? Please," she pleaded. "Think about it."

"Yes." The maid walked to the table and grabbed what appeared to be a missive. "Here."

She accepted it with reservation. "I'd prefer to be alone while I read it."

"Of course."

She waited until the door closed to untie the leather string that held it closed. She blinked rapidly as she stared at the near empty page. A single runic symbol caught her eye.

The meaning wasn't lost on her; in the ancient scrolls from

the Northlands she'd studied with her father, the symbol for need and unfulfilled desire had appeared often enough for her to remember it.

Dearest God. She folded the delicate page and stared heavenward. Last night had been incredible, more than she ever expected. The joining of a man and woman's bodies was undoubtedly a gift. No wonder the monks preached against it unless a couple was married. The powerful emotions that welled up inside her just thinking about it threatened her sanity and faith. Why couldn't he stay here with her? Why hadn't he offered to take her home to Norway?

She knew he loved her. After they'd coupled a third time, he pulled her into his arms and held her close, his strong heartbeat lolling her to sleep like a gentle song.

Those kinds of feelings didn't manifest from nowhere.

The symbol represented everything she felt, too. She placed the letter aside and walked to the door and opened it. "Saga?"

"Yes?"

"Bring your brother Gunnar to me. Please."

Moments later, he entered her room looking anxious. "You wanted to see me?"

"Aye," she said. "What I'm about to discuss with you requires complete honesty from both of us."

He nodded. "Is this about our betrothal?"

"The one our master never announced."

"He departed sooner than we expected, leaving instructions with my father on how to manage the farm until his brother arrives."

"And not a word about us."

"No."

"I don't love you, Gunnar. And I'm sure you don't love me."

His green eyes narrowed. "I could learn to love you," he said graciously, obviously sparing her the humiliation of a direct no.

"I will forever be indebted to you and your family for showing me such kindness and acceptance. But there is something you should know. I am no longer a maiden. Jarl Konal and I..."

"It makes no difference to me," he said. "Tis an honor for any woman to warm the bed of our jarl."

"I understand," she said. "But my feelings will never change. I offered my body willingly to the man I love—the one I wish to call husband."

"He is gone, milady. Tis better to accept it. I will give you what time you need to get used to the idea of marrying me. I swore to protect you. An oath I will never break."

"I am not the sort of woman who accepts defeat easily. Something I learned after meeting Jarl Konal. What I ask for now will require you to fulfill the very vow you made to our master."

He inhaled deeply, looking as if he knew what she was going to say next.

"Take me to the place where his father's longship is anchored. Let me speak with him a last time. If he rejects me, I will return here and marry you without complaint."

Gunnar rubbed his chin, staring intently at her. "I have your word? You won't make my life miserable if we are married? We will live in peace and have children as all husbands and wives do?"

"I swear on my own life." Whatever it was worth without Konal, she didn't know.

"Come," he said. "We have a long ride ahead of us."

KONAL LOWERED THE heavy bag filled with amber onto the boat. He'd waited over a year to stand in this very spot, to feel a longship sway upon the waves again, to feel the salt air breeze in his hair, and to hear the screech of the seagulls overhead.

But no matter how much joy it brought him, his heart was, once again, hollow. Perhaps this is what death felt like, walking about void of emotions. What man wished to take a breath if he couldn't love? By choosing to leave his sweet Silvia behind, he condemned himself to a life of emptiness. The price he must pay to go home.

He returned to the beach and helped load several more barrels onto the ship, supplies for the journey, and his share of the gold and silver he'd earned during his year of service to Prince Ivarr. He'd buy his own steading in the Trondelag, perhaps a parcel of land on one of the barrier islands where he could walk the shoreline every morning and gaze across the North Sea, hoping to catch sight of the woman he loved—soon to be wed to another man.

The reality of it strangled him.

"Konal," one of the guards called.

"What is it?"

"On the cliffs."

Konal looked where the man was pointing. Three hundred feet above them, a couple people were waving their arms wildly. Why didn't they take the footpath down to the water?

Then he heard her soft voice carried on the breeze. "K.O.N.A.L."

Instinctively, he reacted as any man in love would, sprinting up the incline like a wild stallion. She waited with Gunnar, unashamed that she'd, once again, disobeyed him.

"Will you ever listen to me, woman?"

"Only if you send me away."

With anguish in her eyes, she stayed silent.

"Gunnar," he said. "Go below and help my father's men load

the ship."

"Aye." He walked away.

"Did you get the missive?"

She reached inside her cloak and produced the letter. "If this is how you feel..."

"It is."

"Do you love me, Konal?"

With all his heart. More than life itself. More than the gods who ruled his brutal world. He'd wander aimlessly for an eternity, caught between the nine realms, for another night with Silvia. "Aye," he said, bringing a fist to his heart. "I love you. I want you. I need you."

Tears filled her eyes. "Then why did you leave without saying goodbye?"

"Because I know the pain of leaving behind a land you love. And I didn't have the heart to make you suffer any more. At least on the farm, you'd be near your home, maybe one day able to visit the places and people you care for."

"Is that the only reason?"

"No," he admitted. "I didn't have the courage to tell you. I loved before, and that woman cost me more than you'll ever know. But you, sweet Silvia..." He closed the distance between them and caressed her cheek. "You changed me—changed everything. With you, I dare to live again. No longer half a man."

His chest clenched as he realized how much of his soul he'd revealed. For so long, he'd relied only on himself—keeping his family at arm's length, letting his bad temper rule his life. No longer. He'd risk it all one last time for love. "Come with me," he said. "Leave this war ravaged island behind and start a new life with me in Norway. It won't be easy, Silvia. My father will disapprove of our marriage at first. But in time, I hope he'll grow to love you as I do."

"Because I'm a thrall?"

"No," he said. "Because you're a Saxon."

She gazed over his shoulder. "I've never sailed before," she said timidly. "Will I…"

"You're free, Silvia."

She closed her eyes and raised her chin. "Free as the wind," she cried. "Free as your ship upon the water." Then she focused on him again. "Finally free to love you."

Throwing herself into his arms, they both dropped to their knees, clinging to each other.

"Will you be my wife?"

"Yes, Jarl Konal."

Not needing to hear another word, he lifted her into his arms and carried her to the longship, his most precious cargo.

Made in the USA
Columbia, SC
06 October 2021